BIGGLES FLIES AGAIN

BIGGLES FLIES AGAIN

By

CAPT. W. E. JOHNS

By arrangement with

THE THAMES PUBLISHING CO.

LONDON

MADE AND PRINTED IN GREAT BRITAIN BY PURNELL AND SONS, LTD.
PAULTON (SOMERSET) AND LONDON

603 03402 0

CONTENTS

CHAPTER I

THE GOLD RUSH

As THE tropic sun sunk slowly in the west, a thin miasma of mist began to curl upward from the still, silent pool around which the mangroves lifted their gnarled trunks on fantastic stilt-like roots from the slime of the swamp. At one spot, in vivid contrast to the sombre desolation around, a spray of orchids sprang like a flame from a gaunt, low-hanging branch, and mirrored their scarlet beauty in the ebony surface of the water below. Nothing moved; the scene was as lifeless as a picture. Even the air, heavy with the stench of decay and corruption, was still; it hung like a tangible substance over the place and endowed its primeval loneliness with an atmosphere of sinister foreboding.

In the deep shade at the edge of the lagoon, its nose almost touching a rank growth of purple-blotched fungus, an aircraft floated motionless on its own inverted image. At first glance it appeared to be a flying-boat, but mud-coated wheels, now raised high into the wings near the weather-soiled hull, revealed it to be of the amphibian class.

A gunshot split the sun-drenched silence from somewhere near at hand, and, as if in answer, a figure rose slowly from the pilot's seat and stared in the direction from which the sound had come. Simultaneously, as if they were connected in some unseen way, several pieces of what appeared to be bark, floating on the water, sank swiftly, leaving faint ripples to mark their going.

"I wonder what he's got today," said the pilot to someone inside the cabin. The voice echoed eerily over the water.

The person to whom he had spoken emerged from the cabin and seated himself on the edge of the hull near the other.

"I'll tell you, Algy," said the newcomer in a tone of voice which left no possible room for doubt; "it'll be another warty lizard. Maybe it will have a blue belly, for a change, but that makes no difference to the flavour; yellow, red, green—they all taste alike. Smyth will come to the edge of the water, just there"—he pointed to the tiny promontory of mud beside which the machine was moored—"and he'll say, 'Sorry, sir, but this is the best I can do today!' "

"Well, that'll be better than alligator," replied the first speaker. "I'm about sick of alligator. I never want to eat another."

James Bigglesworth, late R.A.F., eyed his companion grimly. "You've only to slip into the water here, once, and they'll do the eating, for a change," he observed dryly. "This place swarms with the brutes."

The mud-stained figure of a third man appeared, picking his way carefully to the edge of the trees. In his right hand he held a gun; in the left he carried a large lizard by the tail.

"Sorry, sir," he said, "but this is the best I can do today."

"That's not so bad. What did you expect to get, a brace of partridges?" grinned Bigglesworth, more often known to his friends as "Biggles". "Get a fire going; it will be time to grouse when we have to eat them raw. I've only one or two matches left."

"I'm eating no raw lizzies," muttered Algernon Montgomery Lacey, Biggles's war-time comrade-at-arms, with conviction. "If the boat doesn't show up by dawn tomorrow, I'm through, and the Oil Investment Company of British Guiana can buzz off and do its own flying," he added viciously, picking up the lizard's tail which Smyth had skinned, and throwing it into a soot-corroded frying-pan.

Biggles nodded. "I'm with you. She's over a month late; there's something wrong somewhere. We'll go down to Georgetown tomorrow and see what it is. I'm all against leaving a job in the middle, but they can't expect us to go on without stores or petrol. We've just about enough left to get to Georgetown; I'm not going to use that up here and walk back. It will evaporate if we sit still, so we might as well go down the coast. If the Agent starts a song and dance about us using the Company's precious petrol, I'll tell him to produce my pay-cheque and do his own aviating."

Actually, the pilot of the three airmen was serious. Biggles had followed up an advertisement which led to his employment by the Oil Investment Company of British

Guiana as a pilot, with the task of photographing from the air likely oil-bearing terrain in the hinterland of north-east tropical America.

The Company had allowed him to choose his own equipment and crew, with the result that he had sought out Algy Montgomery Lacey, formerly of his squadron, as second pilot, and Smyth, his late flight-sergeant-fitter, as general mechanic. And so it came about that six months later they were pursuing their task in a Vickers "Vandal" Amphibian, which they were able to land on the rivers and lagoons among the mangrove swamps near the coast.

Their present rendezvous had been established as a base at which they were to be supplied with stores, oil, and petrol by special boat from Georgetown, and to which they were to hand their reports and the plates they had exposed.

For six months all went well, and the boat had arrived regularly according to plan. Then came a long delay in which they had been reduced to starvation rations before the boat had belatedly put in an appearance with considerably less than the usual stock of provisions Further, their pay-cheques had not been delivered for endorsement, as hitherto, in order that they might be paid into the bank at Georgetown, by the Company's Agent. That was more than two months ago, and they were now reduced to the desperate expedient of living by their gun in a land where, apparently, only reptiles and insects existed. With a philosophy born of war-time experience they made the best of a bad job, daily expecting the arrival of the boat, and, although they had not discussed the reason of its failure to bring the badly-needed supplies, a shrewd suspicion was rapidly forming in Biggles's mind.

II

It did not greatly surprise him therefore when, the following evening, the Agent confirmed it.

"Yes, Bigglesworth," he said, "the Company went into liquidation more than three months ago—and that is all there is to say," he added, with an air of finality.

"Is it?" said Biggles, eyeing the little pock-marked mulatto grimly. "Who told you it was? What about our pay?"

The man made a gesture more eloquent than words.

"I see," said Biggles slowly; "the money dried up, eh? You knew that; you knew that we were stranded up on that hell-bound, fever-smitten coast, yet you hadn't the decency to send word that you were not sending a boat."

"You would hardly expect me to stand the expense of that myself——"

"No. Having seen you, I wouldn't," replied Biggles, breathing heavily. "Did you pay our last cheques into the bank?"

"Yes, but——"

"Come on; but what?"

"Unfortunately there was not sufficient credit at the bank to meet them. They were returned; I have them here."

"What about your own—was that met?"

"Well, yes; you see, being on the spot——"

"You were able to keep ours back until yours was cleared, eh? Well, what are you going to do about it?"

"Do about it?"

"Don't pretend you're a blooming parrot; there's enough outside; you heard what I said. How are we going to get home?"

"I guess that's your own affair," replied the Agent brusquely, turning to some papers on his desk as if the interview was closed.

"Then you're a darn bad guesser," snarled Biggles, taking off his jacket.

"What are you going to do?" cried the Agent, in alarm, turning pale under his yellow skin.

"That's what I asked you," said Biggles harshly.

"What do you want me to do?"

"As far as I can see there's only one thing you can do," replied Biggles through his teeth, taking a pace forward, "and that is to make over that machine in the harbour to us in lieu of pay."

"Preposterous! I have no authority——"

"To blazes with authority; you've got a Company stamp. Get busy and date the deed the day before the Company filed its petition; your clerk can witness it. If you don't," went on the pilot, clenching his fists, "I'm going to give myself the satisfaction of tearing your dirty little gizzard out of your neck and throwing it outside to the dogs."

The Agent opened his mouth to speak, looked up at the airman's face, changed his mind, took up a sheet of headed notepaper, and wrote rapidly.

Five minutes later the pilot, with the deed in his pocket, made his way back to the harbour, where Algy and Smyth were busily engaged scrubbing down the amphibian.

"Company's gone broke; there's no money, but we've got the boat," he told them briefly.

"What's the use of that; are you thinking of flying it back non-stop to London?" sneered Algy sarcastically, mopping his face with an oily rag.

Biggles shook his head. "It was that or nothing," he said, shrugging his shoulders. "We might, by giving joy-rides, work our way up the coast to New Orleans or across to Jamaica, where we could sell her for enough to pay our passages back."

"Jungle Airways Limited, Joy Rides for Niggers, Flip-Flaps for Cannibals," grinned Algy.

"That's about it," agreed Biggles. "Can you think of anything better?"

"No, unless we can borrow that." He nodded towards a spick-and-span white-painted steam-yacht that swung at anchor a hundred yards away.

"Let's talk sense," said Biggles impatiently. "We've enough money for some petrol and handbills to give us a start; we'll see about it tomorrow."

"Pardon me, gentlemen!"

Biggles swung on his heel to face the speaker, and then stared at him curiously, for at first glance it would have been difficult to guess the nationality of the man who had interrupted their conversation. He spoke English like an American, but with the halting lisp peculiar to the Oriental; his face, wide and rather flat, was dominated by the eyes, which were small and dark—beady, as Algy afterwards described them—like those of a doll, but brilliant in their intensity as they flashed from one to the other of the three airmen.

"Yes, what can I do for you?" asked Biggles civilly.

"You are pilots of the airplane, eh? I should like to speak with you privately," was the quickly spoken reply.

"Go ahead," replied Biggles; "we're the pilots and we've plenty of time."

"But not here," replied the man, glancing around. "Follow me," and, turning, he hurried away down a side street.

"What a queer fish," muttered Algy; "but we might as well hear what he has to say."

Their new acquaintance was evidently a believer in the old adage "Walls have ears", for, contrary to their expectations, he did not stop at any of the small eating-houses, but disappeared behind a clump of tree-ferns on the outskirts of the town, where they found him awaiting them. It struck Biggles that he seemed nervous and ill at ease, for it was some moments before he could find words to begin.

"You are Englishmen, eh?" he said at last.

"We are," replied Biggles. "Is that what you wanted to tell us?"

"I think you are to be trusted," muttered the man, ignoring the mild sarcasm. "Listen; I have a secret; you can help me." He dropped his voice to a whisper. "Would you like gold—much gold?"

"Much! More than that if you've got it; it makes nice compact ballast," grinned Biggles. "Where is it?"

"I will tell you—but not now," was the quick answer.

"I knew there was a catch in it," moaned Algy.

"No catch. I have map. Wrecked ship, a Drake ship on the Spanish Main, he said——"

"Who said?" asked Biggles curiously.

"Never mind—I don't know," muttered the man nervously, and it struck Biggles that the words "he said" had slipped out accidentally. "The ship is on the beach; could you land your airplane on a beach, eh?" he continued, looking anxiously at Biggles, whom he evidently assumed to be the leader of the party.

"We could," agreed the pilot.

"Good! We will go shares, one half for me and one half for you three, eh?"

"That's fair enough," nodded Biggles. "Where is it and when do we start? There's no sense in letting it get rusty."

"I will show you in the morning—I shall be with you."

"In the morning?" echoed Biggles in surprise. "How far away is this yellow dross?"

"Hundred miles; perhaps little more."

"Can't be done," said Biggles sadly, shaking his head. "We haven't enough petrol and we've no money to get more."

"I give money," replied the man at once. "I give plenty money. You have gas all ready to start at dawn. Take a shovel and tools for digging."

"Here, wait a minute; let me get this right," muttered Biggles. "You know where some gold is hidden in an old wreck?"

"Yes—yes."

"You'll give us half if we fetch it——"

"No—all fetch it; I come too."

"All right. If we get this gold we split it two ways; you pay expenses and we'll be ready to start at dawn. Is that it?"

"Yes, exactly, but keep secret; other people are on the trail. But how do you say—first come, first serve, eh?"

"Certainly. That is, supposing this job's on the level," said Biggles earnestly, looking the man straight in the eyes. "I'm not doing any bank-busting or bootlegging."

"No, no, all square. Here, take this; be ready at dawn. Bring tools and food. We may be one day or two." He thrust some notes into Biggles's hand and hurried away towards the town.

"Tell me," murmured Algy weakly, "am I dreaming or do we start on a treasure-hunt tomorrow?"

"We do," grinned Biggles, "and we may never get another chance. I'm not altogether infatuated with this customer; he looks a bit queer, but it struck me that he knew what he was talking about. Come on, though; let's see about getting the petrol; it'll be dark in half an hour."

III

"Here he comes!" Biggles, leaning over the side of the "Vandal", flung the words back over his shoulder to Algy, who was peering into the early-morning haze on the other side of the machine. A canoe, paddled by a negro, bumped alongside, and their acquaintance of the previous evening scrambled aboard. He flung the boatman a coin and turned to Biggles.

"We go," he said in a sibilant hiss. "Waste no time."

His face was pale, and he was panting as if he had been running; Biggles glanced significantly at Algy as he dropped into his seat.

Biggles started up the engine, which broke the silence with its powerful roar. As he sat back to allow it to warm up he looked around for the stranger and saw him peering anxiously out of the cabin-window at the quickly forming group of natives on the bank.

"You'd better come and sit next to me," he called; "you've got to show me the way."

Obediently the passenger crawled through the small cabin door into the vacant seat next to the pilot, which was normally occupied by Algy.

"You'll have to stay in the cabin with Smyth," Biggles told his second pilot apologetically.

He glanced at the thermometer, raced the engine for a moment, and then taxied quickly towards the open water near the harbour mouth. When he saw that he had a clear run he pushed the throttle open and soared through the screaming gulls towards the turquoise-blue sky above. For a few minutes he circled widely, climbing steadily for height, and then nudged his companion, who was looking over the side with an expression of mingled surprise and apprehension on his face.

"Which way?" he yelled.

For answer the man thrust a sketch-map into his hand.

The pilot set the machine on even keel and allowed it to fly "hands off" while he examined the map closely. He had become sufficiently familiar with the coast to recognize the locality instantly; it was the delta of the Orinoco. In a backwater of the mighty estuary a spot was marked in red; he glanced at his companion, who was watching him anxiously, and raised his eyebrows inquiringly, with his finger on the spot. The man nodded. Biggles handed him back the map, which he no longer needed, and set his course north-west to follow the coast-line he knew so well. He throttled back to three-quarter throttle and settled himself down for a two-hours' cruise.

On his right lay the deep green of the Atlantic, sweeping away until it kissed the horizon in the infinite distance. Below, an irregular white line marked where the surf waged eternal war on the broad belt of silvery sand. To the left, the dark, untrodden forest lay like a great stain between sea and sky until it melted at last into the purple haze of the dim beyond. There was little risk of losing the way, and except for keeping the nose of the machine on the unmistakable white surf-line by an occasional touch on the rudder-bar the pilot had little to do. The time passed slowly, but at last the breakers curled round to the east, and when the mouth of the mighty river lay before them he throttled back and commenced a long glide towards the backwater that was their destination.

Reaching it, he circled once very low to make sure there were no obstructions, then sank lightly on to the still water and taxied up the silvery, sandy beach into the shade of a clump of coconut palms. He switched off, and climbed out. A humming bird hovered over the nose of the machine for an instant, and then darted towards a clump of exotic flowers that thrust themselves above the undergrowth near the edge of the forest.

"Nice spot," Biggles observed approvingly as he glanced around. "Where do we start digging?"

The tropical beauty of the scene was evidently lost on their passenger, for no sooner had their wheels touched the shore than he leapt lightly to the ground and hurried along the strip of beach, looking eagerly to right and left. He stopped suddenly and waved to them triumphantly.

"Here it is!" he shouted.

Hurrying to the spot, the airmen examined the cause of his excitement dubiously. It was a piece of charred wood protruding from the sand. Several similar pieces formed a rough curve.

"They're the bones of a ship, no doubt of that; burnt to the water's edge, by the look of it," observed Biggles. "Let's get the spades."

Two hours later he paused to wipe the perspiration from his face. "Phew!" he gasped. "We shall have to steady the pace a bit. There's more sand here than meets the eye."

Algy straightened his back stiffly. "Where does it all come from anyway? I didn't know there was so much sand in the world," he observed, gloomily.

A glance around the scene of their labours revealed the truth of Biggles's words. For two hours they had shovelled sand madly aside, without pause and with hardly a word, but the only visible result was four great holes exposing still more sand. The ribs around which they had been working showed a little more of their length, that was all.

"Let's knock off for a bit," he suggested. "The stuff's been here for five hundred years, so another minute or two shouldn't hurt it."

They returned to the machine, unpacked some provisions, and with difficulty persuaded their passenger to desist and join them in a frugal meal. A few minutes later they resumed their task, digging feverishly into the yielding but heavy sand. By sunset the holes were appreciably deeper, but there was still no sign of anything but sand.

"Hullo! What's this?" Algy bent forward and eagerly picked up a small, roughly-round object that lay at his feet. The others were around him instantly, examining the find with intense interest.

Algy rubbed the disc vigorously on the seat of his trousers and then held it up again for inspection. It was undoubtedly a coin of some sort, and an inscription was faintly legible.

"Phillipofour, one-six-two-one," he read slowly, and turned it over. Amongst a mass of hieroglyphics two castles could be distinguished. "What the dickens is it?" he asked.

"Piece of eight; eight reales—a silver coin minted in Peru in sixteen twenty-one," explained the passenger blandly.

"You seem to know all about it," said Biggles, quickly.

"I have seen them before."

"Well, let's find some more; silver is better than nothing," observed the pilot, picking up his spade.

But the sun dropped over the horizon with tropical suddenness and they had no choice but to return to the "Vandal" to make preparations for the night. A faint hum, slowly increasing in volume, became audible in the still air.

"Here come the enemy," said Biggles dryly.

"Enemy! Where?" The passenger sprang to his feet in alarm and stared out over the sea.

"Are you expecting them to come that way?" asked the pilot evenly. "I was talking about mosquitoes," he added. "We'd better oil ourselves or we shall be torn to pieces."

IV

Biggles, dreaming that he had been seized by an alligator, sat bolt upright under the wing of the machine where he had made his bed, and gazed stupidly at a circle of hostile faces glaring at him. He yawned, shifted his gaze to where the rising sun had turned the sheltered stretch of water into a pool of carmine and gold, and smiled grimly as his eyes fell on a yacht standing close in to the shore. He recognized it for the one he had last seen in the harbour at Georgetown. A dinghy was drawn up on the beach.

"So here you are," he smiled.

"Quit grinning and get on your feet," snarled a man in sailor's uniform, evidently the leader of the shore party.

Algy lazily opened one eye and then sat bolt upright as if he had been stung by a scorpion. "Good heavens!" he gasped. "What's all this?"

"Come on, step out, baby," snapped the man in uniform, drawing an automatic.

"You'll hurt yourself with that thing one of these days," observed Biggles seriously, as he rolled out from under the wing-tip and stood up, yawning. "What a lovely day."

What followed happened so quickly that even Algy, who was prepared for something of the sort, could hardly believe it. Biggles's right hand shot out and slashed a handful of sand straight into the man's eyes. He leapt sideways like a cat as the automatic exploded, and then forward; his left hand took the man in the pit of the stomach, and as he doubled up with a gasping groan Biggles, the automatic in his hand, swung up to face the rest just as they started forward. They stopped dead as they saw the squat muzzle covering them.

"Well, and now what is it all about?" he asked coldly. "Have you bought this place or——?"

His voice died in his throat as, glancing to one side, his eyes fell on a vision of blonde loveliness standing beside an elderly man in white ducks.

"I beg your pardon, madam," he went on when he had recovered from his surprise, "for this unseemly bickering; I had no idea——" He tossed the weapon carelessly into the undergrowth and turned to the man beside the girl. "Having disturbed my party, sir, may I suggest that you introduce yourself and state your business in a manner less suggestive of the methods employed by the gentlemen who once frequented this coast," he concluded icily.

"My name is Hollinger, Cyrus P. Hollinger, of Tonville, Illinois, U.S.A.," replied the man, looking rather uncomfortable.

"Mine's Biggelsworth—James C. Biggelsworth, of nowhere in particular," replied Biggles lightly. "Meet my young and irresponsible friend, the Honourable Algernon Montgomery Lacey, of Merioneth Towers, Merioneth, Merionethshire; if you don't believe it you can ask him yourself. Algy, allow me to introduce you to Mr. Hollinger and—may I presume?—thank you—Miss Hollinger. I fear I cannot offer you much in the way of hospitality," he went on, "but we have some good coffee."

"That's fine," broke in Mr. Hollinger, "but where is that rascally steward of mine?"

"Steward, was he?" nodded Biggles. "To tell you the truth, I don't know where he is. He went off to sleep by himself, but I fancy he must have seen you coming."

Mr. Hollinger dismissed his crew, and over an excellent breakfast on the beach, supplied by the ship's galley, the story soon unfolded itself.

"He must have overheard me discussing the wreck with my daughter," exclaimed Mr. Hollinger, "and the sight of your aircraft gave him the idea of slipping along first—and he might have got away with it, too, had there been anything to take."

"But isn't there some gold here?" asked Biggles quickly.

"There should be, but I've made a hobby of hunting these things out all my life and I've never found any yet."

"Do you mean to say I've shifted all that sand for nothing?" cried Algy, aghast.

"I shouldn't be surprised," laughed the American. "By the way, what are you boys doing with an airplane in this out-of-the-way part of the world?"

Briefly, Biggles explained what had happened, and the old man listened in amazement to his story, laughing loudly at Algy's interpolated comments on the character of the Oil Investment Company of British Guiana.

"Well, it was a blow to lose our pay," Biggles concluded, "but it's some satisfaction to know that we've done the Company out of the machine."

Mr. Hollinger laughed, it seemed to Biggles immoderately, at the story of how it had been obtained. "Well, let's go and see if there's anything worth salving in the wreck," exclaimed the American at last, rising.

Many hands soon made light work of the operations, and by evening the skeleton of the once proud ship lay stark and gaunt on the beach. They found nothing, not a coin or a relic of any description. Algy's piece of eight was the sum total of the proceeds.

"My word, I'm glad you turned up," breathed Algy fervently to Isobel Hollinger, as he looked at the huge excavation. "If I'd done that and got nothing at the end of it I should have crawled away and given myself up to the alligators."

"Yes, it is disappointing," admitted Mr. Hollinger, "particularly as by coming here I have missed the chance of a big deal. I should have been in Peru by the twentieth and it's the fifteenth now. Can't be done."

"Where do you want to go?" asked Biggles suddenly.

"Lima."

"Lima! Speaking from memory, that is a fair step from here, but it might be done," said Biggles.

"Impossible! My yacht only steams at twenty knots."

"What about that?" Biggles pointed to the "Vandal".

"Say! I never thought of it," muttered Mr. Hollinger. "I wonder how far it is?"

"I'm not thinking so much of the distance as of the difficulty of getting fuel on the way," said Biggles, as they made their way to the dinghy in order to examine the map in the chart-room of Hollinger's yacht, the *Sea Dream*. "We've an endurance range of about seven hundred miles, and we could carry some spare fuel with us. We can follow the Pan American route via Port of Spain, Maracaibo, and Panama, and then down the other side via Buenaventura, I believe it goes. It's about three thousand five hundred miles, for a rough guess, and, bar accidents, we could do it if we started at dawn tomorrow."

"I'll risk it; the yacht can follow on!" cried the American enthusiastically. "I'll pay expenses and a thousand dollars if you get me through."

"Good!" cried Biggles delightedly. "Come on, Algy, let's run over the machine and slip down to Georgetown for a full load of fuel."

Just before noon, four days later, the "Vandal" touched its wheels lightly on Las Palmas aerodrome at Barranco, near Lima.

"Well, you boys, I'm very much obliged to you," smiled Mr. Hollinger as he climbed out of the machine and handed Biggles an envelope. "Here are the dollars I promised you, and the pay-cheques you failed to receive from the Oil Company."

"Pay-cheques!" exclaimed Biggles in surprise. "What's that got to do with you?"

"I'm the managing director," grinned Hollinger, backing away. "I suspected our Agent in Georgetown was crooked, so I ran down to see. That's really why I was there. See you later!"

CHAPTER 2

THE MAID AND THE MOUNTAINS

BIGGLES leaned back in his chair on the *patio* of the Hotel Guibert, in La Paz, and watched with interest a line of grunting llamas toiling across the cobbled *plaza*. A mule, followed by an *arriero* and a string of curses, which sounded to Biggles adequate, even though their meaning was quite beyond him, threaded its way in the opposite direction. Its load was continually shifting, and constant stops had to be made to re-hitch.

"I'm glad that chap isn't my rigger," he observed, moodily, as the *arriero* halted the beast for the third time within ten yards.

The scene had become familiar, for more than a month had elapsed since they had landed on the Pacific side of the South American continent. For a fortnight they had flown Mr. Hollinger to various points of the compass on business before he departed, profuse in thanks, to the *Sea Dream*, which was lying at anchor off Pisco.

Biggles, remembering that Wilkinson, once "Wilks" of 287 Squadron, R.A.F., was now pilot-instructor to the Bolivian Air Force, would not hear of returning to Europe without looking him up, so after the necessary formalities had been arranged by the British Consular Agent they had flown the "Vandal" across the frontier to the Bolivian Air Force aerodrome at Alto de la Paz, to the great delight of Wilks. They had taken up quarters at the Guibert, where they foregathered each evening to discuss past exploits and future prospects.

"How are you getting on with your Spanish?" asked Wilkinson, with a wink at Algy.

"*Muy bien, gracias amigo,*" grinned Biggles, for he had been amusing himself by learning the language of the country. "I got on very well in the market this morning; I bought a *poncho** for a souvenir. By the way, what is all this talk I hear about a fellow named Estaban? I couldn't quite get the hang of it, and when I asked people they just shut up like oysters."

"Good heavens, man, don't tell me that you haven't heard that Estaban Martinez has kidnapped the President's daughter?"

"What's she like?" asked Algy, sitting up and taking interest in the conversation.

"Consuelo Guardia has the reputation of being the most beautiful girl in Spanish America," replied Wilkinson respectfully, "in fact, she's a wizard," he added fervently, with a disregard for niceties.

"Great Scott! Why hasn't somebody fetched her back? Come on; let's go," cried Algy, rising.

"Don't be a fool—sit down," Wilkinson told him quickly, dropping his voice and glancing around. "You'll

* *A blanket-like garment with a hole cut for the head, so that it forms a cloak; worn by the working-class in Bolivia.*

get a knife in your back if you go around shouting like that."

"Tell me about it," pleaded Algy, earnestly.

"Estaban is one big brigand chief," whispered Wilkinson, "and then some. He looks like a comic-opera star turn, but that's where the funny stuff ends; there's nothing humorous in Estaban's make-up, believe me."

"Where does he hang out?" inquired Biggles.

"That doesn't help," replied Wilkinson, shaking his head. "They know pretty well where his headquarters are. Look; you see the mountain over there?" He nodded towards a gigantic white peak in the distance. "That's Mount Illimani—the Great Mother, it means, and it's venerated by every Indian in Bolivia. Well, his place is somewhere behind there, but don't forget those mountains roll back for about three hundred miles until they fall down in the Amazon valley. Estaban rules the district like a prince by collecting toll and ransom from travellers who have to go through the *apacheta* to the *altiplanicia*, that is, through the pass to the high sierras beyond; there are several mines up there, mostly tin."

"Why don't they send troops to turf him out of it?" asked Biggles, in puzzled surprise.

"Can't be done," said Wilkinson, shaking his head. "The British army could lose itself in those mountains and it would take another army months to find them. You can't cross those hills without a train of llamas or mules, and Estaban would know you were on your way before you left the town. La Paz is alive with spies. The fellow has been a curse for years, but he has never tried anything on this scale before. Poor old Don Jaime, the President, is nearly off his head; he worships the girl. Estaban is asking for a ransom of two hundred and fifty thousand bolivianos and Don Jaime says he hasn't got it; I don't suppose he has—he hasn't been in office long enough. He's offered a reward of ten thousand bolivianos for the girl, and the Government has offered ten thousand for Estaban's body, dead or alive, but they are pretty safe; they might as well have offered a million, for all the chance they have of getting him. No one could get within ten miles of his *estancia*. They talk about getting up a public subscription."

"But they must have some idea, to within a mile or so, where Estaban hangs out," returned Biggles.

"Come up to the map-room at the aerodrome tomorrow and I'll show you to within two hundred square miles, and that's as much as anyone can tell you," replied Wilkinson, "but don't you try doing anything foolish," he muttered darkly. "An Aymara Indian couldn't get across those hills, so it's no use you trying."

Biggles nibbled the end of a match-stalk reflectively. "It seems a pity," he observed slowly.

II

The following morning he examined with interest the big map in the pilots' room at the aerodrome. A pencil line, drawn by Wilkinson, enclosed an oblong-shaped area roughly twenty miles long by ten miles deep.

"It's generally supposed that Estaban's *estancia* is somewhere about there, but, of course, no one knows for certain," he told them.

"I see," said Biggles vaguely. "Well, it looks rough country to me and I don't think I shall wear out any shoe-leather looking for Consuelo. Come on, Algy, we had better run over the machine; she'll need an overhaul before we leave."

"Where's Smyth?" he went on, with a change of tone, when they were out of earshot.

"He's cleaning the machine. Why?"

"Good. Is the camera still aboard?"

"Yes."

"We still have plenty of unexposed plates, haven't we?"

"Plenty."

"Fine! Let's do a little reconnaissance."

A few minutes later the "Vandal" was in the air, climbing as quickly as possible for height. Progress was slow, for the aerodrome at Alto de la Paz is situated fourteen thousand feet above sea-level, considerably higher than the normal ceiling of a civil aircraft. For this reason Smyth had been left behind in order to lighten the load as far as possible, and with Biggles at the controls Algy was ready to operate the camera.

When they were five thousand feet above the aerodrome the pilot struck off at a tangent and headed towards the snowy crest of Mount Illimani. As they neared it he edged away towards the lower peaks on the right, but even so he had not much more than a few hundred feet to spare when he slipped across them and looked ahead for what lay beyond. Something struck the plane with the vibrating crack of a whip-lash, and a small round hole appeared in the lower port plane. Biggles grimaced, and made a mental note that Wilkinson had evidently spoken the truth about Estaban's bodyguard of snipers.

Once over the main range the ground fell away in an awe-inspiring series of lesser ranges. As far as the eye could see, the landscape presented a vista of serrated ridges of rock, torn and split by the torture of innumerable earthquakes, and Biggles realised for the first time the difficulty of his task. Something caught his eye and he changed his course slightly towards it. It was a lake, one of those peculiar to the Andean range, situated thousands of feet above sea-level. It was near the end of a large plateau, bleak and stony and broken by occasional patches of *tola* scrub.

"What a place!" he mused. And then a movement attracted his attention and he peered down intently. Sheep? No, llamas, he thought, and stared at a group of animals grazing on the edge of the plateau near the entrance of a small ravine. He pointed, and signalled to Algy to start exposing plates.

For half an hour he flew up and down at the same altitude until every inch of the plateau, the lake, and their environs had been covered by the camera, and then he turned his nose back towards the aerodrome.

For the rest of the day they worked hard, Biggles and Smyth developing and printing the plates, Algy mounting them up together on a large white card. When he had finished, a single photograph was made of the whole and a bird's-eye picture of the valley lay before them.

"If he's in the area Wilks marked out, he is here," said Biggles, laying a finger on the photograph, after a minute examination. "A lizard couldn't find a foothold anywhere else. Here is the pass." He traced a faint wavering line with the point of his pencil. "From the machine it seemed to lose itself on the plateau, but you can still faintly see it in the photograph. Here it goes, straight across. Now look over here in the corner; notice how all these small tracks converge on that point, and that is where the llamas were. The vertical photograph only shows rock and a tiny fissure, but I should say the rock overhangs a canyon, and that is where Estaban and his friends must hang out. Do you think you could land the 'Vandal' on that lake, Algy?" he concluded abruptly.

Algy looked up in surprise. "Of course I could."

Biggles nodded. "The thing that worries me most, though," he said, "is whether you could get her off again. It's high up, remember, very high up, and on that flat surface with no wind the 'Vandal' might not unstick."

"She'll come off all right; there is plenty of room and we can dismantle everything we don't need for the job. What's the idea?"

Biggles leaned forward and whispered in his ear for some minutes; when he had finished Algy looked at him dubiously.

"I don't think much of it," he said, very serious for once.

"Well, it sounds all right to me," replied Biggles. "Let's go and find Wilks."

They found him in his office, checking up and signing log-books.

"Have you got a parachute here, Wilks?" asked Biggles quietly.

"No. Why?"

"Oh, I just wondered."

"Wait a minute. I believe there is a sample the Irvin people sent down some time ago. It was a special job, extra large, I believe, for high-altitude work, but we didn't buy any."

"Let's see it," demanded Biggles.

Wilks looked at him curiously. "What crazy scheme have you got in your head, now?" he asked.

"Never mind that," replied Biggles. "Get me the brolly, and if your people hear any aviating tonight tell them not to worry. We are going to try an experiment if it's fine."

III

With Algy at the stick, the "Vandal" nosed its way through the night, three thousand feet above the mighty Cordillera, and headed for the plateau. Biggles, looking out, could see the lake clearly, and waved the pilot on a course midway between it and the spot where he had seen the llamas. He stood up, and then started to climb out. Algy throttled back to stalling speed and waved his hand in silent farewell. Biggles remained poised for a moment and then disappeared into the black void below. The pilot turned in a wide circle back towards the aerodrome.

Biggles, plunging downwards, gasped in relief as the parachute opened and his harness took the strain. He looked around curiously. To the right lay the lake; below, the plateau was wrapped in profound darkness and merged into the mountains, whose razor-like peaks, hard-cut against the sky, encircled him. The silence was uncanny; only the distant hum of the "Vandal's" engines reached his ears, and a horrible feeling slowly crept over him that he was not falling, but was hanging suspended in space from some invisible object. Suddenly the black floor of the earth seemed to spring up to meet him.

"Heck!" he gasped, as he sprawled headlong, and then staggered quickly to his feet. But there was no danger of being dragged; the air was still and the silk billowed softly to earth beside him. He removed his harness, folded the parachute roughly into a ball, and thrust it out of sight under a *tola* bush. He then unfastened a bundle from his shoulder and unwrapped the *poncho* he had bought in the market. This he donned, together with one of the round hats worn by the natives, and placing his revolver ready for instant action set off at a brisk pace in the direction of his destination. He made little attempt at concealment, but nevertheless he paused every few minutes to listen.

He had walked for perhaps twenty minutes when a light became visible ahead and he advanced more warily; presently he was able to discern that the light came from the open window of a large *adobe* building which stood at the entrance of the ravine they had marked down on the photo-map. A short distance beyond were several more dim lights and a group of low buildings, which he took to be the *ranchos*, or peons' dwellings. Walking on tiptoe, every nerve alert, he sidled up to the rock wall of the canyon and stood for a moment staring into the darkness, ears strained to catch the slightest sound.

Faint voices and the noise of animals munching came from the direction of the *ranchos*; then somewhere near at hand a man began speaking in a loud voice. Biggles was surprised there were no sentries, and came to the conclusion that the bandit relied on those in the mountains to prevent the approach of strangers. Stealthily he crept nearer to the open window, which he could now see reached to the ground and opened on to the inevitable *patio*. Revolver in hand, he peeped in. Seated at a table in the centre of the room, on which were strewn the remains of a meal, were a man and a girl. The man had his back towards him, but the girl was facing the window, and after the first glance he had no doubt as to her identity. She wore a black mantilla which covered the hair and was draped across the shoulders, enhancing the poise of the proud Castilian head.

The man was talking of ransom and the unpleasant consequences that would follow the refusal of her father to pay, and Biggles's nostrils twitched slightly as he listened and then advanced noiselessly across the room towards the unsuspecting man. The girl did not move; she must have seen him, yet not by a single movement did she betray it.

"One sound, *señor*, and you die," said Biggles coldly. "Keep your hands upon the table."

The Bolivian's head turned slowly. His eyes looked straight into the muzzle of the gun in Biggles's hand and remained fixed on it, as if fascinated.

"*Señorita*, we go," said Biggles quietly.

"*Donde, señor?*"

"To your father." Obediently she rose to her feet. "And you, *señor*, I hesitate to kill you, but I fear I must—unless you would prefer to accompany us?"

Estaban Martinez, accustomed to carry out the threats he promised, did not understand simple bluff. He drew a deep breath, opened his mouth as if to speak, saw Biggles's finger tighten on the trigger, changed his mind, and with an expressive shrug of his shoulders rose to his feet and walked slowly towards the window. Biggles relieved him of his knife and revolver and tossed them into a bush.

"One sound, *señor*, and I shoot," he murmured again as Estaban glanced reflectively towards the *ranchos*. "Let us go to the lake; it looks enchanting in the moonlight."

The bandit bowed and started off in the desired direction, with Biggles and the girl close behind.

They covered a mile in silence while the moon rose and flooded the plateau with silvery radiance. Suddenly Estaban laughed, making it clear that he apprehended no danger from the direction they were taking. It was not a pleasant sound, and the pilot hoped more than ever that his plan would not fail. They reached the edge of the water and he glanced at his luminous wrist-watch. It was only three o'clock; they would have to wait more than two hours for daybreak.

"How long do we stand here?" asked the bandit, after a while. "I have seen this view before; it becomes monotonous."

"I'll show you another presently if you will have

patience—one you've never seen before," Biggles promised him with mock politeness.

"Tomorrow you shall pay for this," returned the bandit venomously.

"Wear this, *señorita*; it grows cold," said Biggles, handing the girl his *poncho*.

"*Gracias, señor*," she whispered, looking in surprise at the semi-military jacket he wore, and which he now exposed for the first time.

The pale glow of the false dawn flooded the eastern sky, faded, and was replaced by the first shafts of light of the true dawn. Slowly the lake turned from black to steely blue. The snowy peaks of the Andean range which towered above them gleamed pink against a pale turquoise sky. The light grew stronger and the mountain tops assumed a more rosy hue in the crystal-clear atmosphere.

Biggles glanced towards the canyon and saw figures moving near the entrance. At the same moment he heard the distant hum of the "Vandal's" engines, and his trained eye picked out a tiny moving speck flashing back the sunlight above the range. The bandit drew in his breath with a sudden hiss of understanding as the distant crackle of rifle-fire reached them.

"The reward offered for your person is the same, dead or alive," said Biggles pointedly, as the bandit crouched low as if to spring; "the choice rests with you." Out of the corner of his eye he saw mounted figures racing towards them from the direction of the canyon, and knew that they had been seen.

But Algy in the "Vandal" had seen them too. He flattened out over the water as near to them as he dared, and the keel of the amphibian cut a long line of creamy foam across the surface of the still water. Without waiting for the machine to finish her run he swung round and taxied swiftly towards them.

"In you go, *señorita*," said Biggles briskly, for the peons were less than a quarter of a mile away, and she waded out into the icy water without a moment's hesitation to where Algy was now waiting at the cabin door to receive her.

Estaban's lips parted in a snarl and he held his ground.

"As you like," said Biggles coldly, raising his revolver and squinting along the barrel.

"Wait!" cried Estaban. "I go," and he followed the girl into the machine, with Biggles close behind. The amphibian surged out into deep water just as the peons reached the bank and raised their rifles. A volley of shots rang out and a bullet glanced off the engine-cowling with a shrill *whang*.

Algy shoved the throttle open viciously, and the "Vandal", gathering speed every second, roared across the lake in a cloud of spray. He was conscious of someone crawling into the seat next to him, but he did not look to see who it was; with set face he was watching the opposite bank rush towards him, and still the machine did not "unstick". White-lipped, he jerked the control column back into his stomach; the "Vandal" lifted itself from the water with an effort and wobbled as if uncertain as to whether to go on or fall back again. For one ghastly moment he thought she was going to stall, but she picked up slowly and rose gracefully into the air. The pilot shuddered; only he knew how close they had been to disaster.

As they climbed slowly towards the peaks now gleaming dazzling white against a brilliant blue sky, he risked a glance at his companion, and started as his eyes met those of the girl. They smiled as their eyes met, and Algy looked towards the mountain ranges with renewed interest.

As they crossed over them several bullets struck the machine. One ripped through the instrument-board and the altimeter flew to pieces in a shower of splinters and broken glass. The girl did not even flinch, and Algy grinned his admiration as he throttled back and began the long glide towards the aerodrome.

As their wheels touched the ground Wilkinson and several officers ran out to meet them, only to stop in stupefied amazement when they saw who was sitting in the fiont seat with the pilot.

"Coffee for four and jump to it!" cried Algy, as he switched off. "The *señorita* is frozen."

"Make it for three," corrected Biggles, emerging from the cabin.

"Why for three?" asked Algy in surprise.

"Estaban won't need any," replied Biggles quietly. "He got his head in the way of one of those slugs as we crossed the mountains. Go and give the President a ring, Wilks; he must be anxious about his daughter."

CHAPTER 3

THE BLUE ORCHID

BIGGLES looked at his companion doubtfully as he stirred his coffee reflectively on the *patio* of the Hotel Guibert in La Paz.

"That's all very well," he said slowly. "We are heroes at the moment and Bolivia belongs to us if we want it. The President has asked us to join the Bolivian Air Force with any rank we like to name, but what about when the next revolution comes along? Don Jaime will lose his job, and so shall we; in fact, we should probably lose our lives as well trying to defend him, because we haven't been brought up to understand that a President is only a very temporary officer, and that unless he grabs what he can and then hoofs it, it is only a matter of time before the crowd kicks him out. Then again, Algy, old son, you can't go on flirting with Consuelo unless you intend marrying her. No, we had better get out while the band is playing jazz, instead of going feet first with the band playing the Dead March."

"And do what?" asked Algy disconsolately. "Go back to England and start an air-taxi show at Heston, or something like that? Not for me. I'm not aviating any ham-fisted pupils through London fogs if I know it."

Biggles turned to the waiter who had entered and halted respectfully a little distance away. "Yes, what is it?" he asked.

The man hurried forward and handed him a card. "Professor J. T. Smilee, F.R.H.S.," read the pilot. "Where is he?—ah!"

He rose to meet an elderly man with a short grey beard who had stepped forward from the shadow. "How d'you do?" said Biggles, smiling. "My name is Bigglesworth—were you looking for me?"

"My name is Smilee," replied their visitor. "I would like to have a few words with you, if I may."

"Do, by all means," replied Biggles. "You sound English. If you are, so much the better. Take a pew and have some coffee—meet Mr. Lacey, my partner."

"Yes, I've just arrived in La Paz, and as the talk of the town is about your recent exploit I thought I would come and see you about an idea which may or may not prove to be practicable."

Biggles raised his eyebrows. "Do you mean something to do with flying?"

"Yes. You see, it is like this. I've come over from Para to look for something which I believe is to be found in the jungle some distance away from here. By travelling overland by mule, and by *balsa* down the rivers, it will take me at least six months to reach the spot, and get back. It struck me that it might be possible for an aeroplane to get there and return in a matter of only two or three days."

"I think you had better tell us the whole story," suggested Biggles; "then we can weigh up the proposition."

"Very well, but I warn you it will sound rather fantastic. I will be as brief as possible; the details can be discussed at leisure afterwards if necessary."

The professor produced a big briar pipe, filled it, and got it going to his satisfaction before he began.

"I am an orchid-hunter, or perhaps it would be better to say a collector, since I work for my own pleasure and not for profit; most of my finds go to Kew," he began. "The story opens some years ago when a native rumour got around in Para of a mysterious blue orchid that had been seen somewhere in the interior. The natives are learning to understand the value of these things. I believe the story actually started at Manaos, which is, as you know, some thousand miles up the Amazon, and it lost nothing in the telling by the time it had reached the mouth of the river. I made allowances for that. Six months ago a halfbreed *picador de goma*—a rubber-collector—working up the Beni river found a *balsa*—which is a local craft used for river transport—drifting downstream. In it was —well, what was left of a man. Examination of the effects revealed him to have been a Mr. F. Hutson, a well-known professional orchid-hunter; but that was not all. In his diary was a note to the effect that he had learnt from a Leco Indian where the blue orchid grew. He had made a rough sketch-map and had written a description of how to find the place. This was probably for his own use. Well, he found the flower."

"How do you know that?" asked Biggles quickly.

"There was one in the boat with him—at least, there was *a* flower. It had shrivelled up, of course, and lost its colour, but the Curator at Kew, to whom it was sent, was unable to identify it with any known species."

"And that's what you're after?"

"Exactly!"

"But I couldn't land in the forest, if that's what you mean!"

"I am well aware of that," replied the Professor quietly, "but I understand your craft is of the type that can land on water. Is that so?"

Biggles nodded.

"Very well. Here is a copy of the sketch-map which Hutson made. Here is the place." He indicated a spot on the map with his finger. "Here is the Beni river. Hutson turned off here—up this tributary, which ends in a fairly large lake. The orchid grows, according to his notes, quite close to the edge of that lake. Unfortunately poor Hutson's entries were made before he had reached the spot, so he does not actually confirm it. He was probably full of fever, but pushed on until he had reached his goal, and then collapsed and died before he even had a chance to write a description of his find."

"I don't like places where people die," observed Algy, shaking his head.

"Well, I admit it is a queer country and one which we know little about," admitted the Professor. "It's full of fever, of course, but that is not likely to affect us in the short time we should be there if we decided to go. If you could land your machine on the lake we should be back in less than a week."

"Have you a proper map of the country besides that sketch-map?" asked Biggles.

The Professor took one out of his case and handed it to Biggles, who made some quick calculations. "It seems to be about three hundred miles each way," he said. "We can carry enough petrol to do that comfortably, but do you realize what a forced landing would mean?"

"That is a risk I am willing to take if you are," observed the Professor. "I am putting this up to you purely as a business deal. I am not a poor man and am willing to pay any reasonable figure for your services. In case of the loss of your machine I am willing to replace it at the earliest possible moment. It would cost a considerable sum of money to reach the place by surface craft, anyway, and the saving of time by air is tremendously important. Moreover, I do not think the risk of a forced landing is worse than the hazards of fever, hostile natives, and the reptiles of the jungle—not to mention the discomfort."

"Well, I'm game," said Biggles shortly. "What about you, Algy?"

Algy nodded. "When do we start?" he said. "I suppose Smyth will come along?"

"He's not likely to be left behind," said Biggles.

II

The first thing that struck Biggles, when, four days later, the keel of the "Vandal" dropped lightly on the water of the unknown lake, was the unusually large number of dead and dying trees on the bank. The surface of the lake, contrary to his expectation, was remarkably free from weed, and this relieved his mind from one anxiety, for he was by no means certain how the machine would behave on a weed-choked surface, and he had no desire to experiment.

Algy held up his head and sniffed the air. "Queer smell about this place," he observed casually, as the pilot began to taxi towards the bank nearest to the spot indicated on the sketch-map. They passed the place where the lake bayed out into the river, and then swept round into a cove which looked as if it might lead to another affluent, but proved to be a *cul de sac.* The pilot taxied right up to the bank, switched off, and stared at the forest. Out of the corner of his eye he could see the others staring, too.

The place was dead. Not a single speck of green caught the eyes. The leafless trees were of a dull grey colour and stood stark and gaunt as if they had been struck by lightning.

"The forest of death," remarked Algy humorously, but the joke seemed to fall flat.

Biggles had noticed something else, and he looked around with a puzzled expression, as if he could not quite make out what it was. When Algy spoke he knew. It was the silence, dead, utter, and absolute—not the lesser noise of a remote rural scene in a civilized country, but an aching silence, a complete absence of sound that worried the eardrums and repelled intrusion. There was no movement; even the mosquitoes were absent. He looked at the bank; the earth was deep with black, rotting vegetation, and the stench of it enveloped them like a blanket.

"I don't like the smell of this place," said Algy, with a change of tone. "Smells like something—can't make it out quite——" His voice echoed eerily and with startling clarity among the silent trees.

The water around them was black and threw back the inverted reflection of the desolation on the bank with artificial intensity. For perhaps three minutes all four of them stood and stared at it.

"Pah! Let's get out of this," said Algy suddenly. "The place reeks of——"

"Of what?" said Smilee in a curious tone.

"Of—of—of death," replied Algy in a queer voice. The words, which appeared to rise unbidden to his lips, seemed to startle him and he shivered suddenly. "Come on, Biggles," he said again; "let's get out of this; there's something about it I don't like, something—unclean."

"Dash it all, Algy, we'll get to the bottom of it now we've come so far," exclaimed Biggles irritably. "What ails the place, anyway?"

Smilee jumped ashore and grabbed at a branch to steady himself. It collapsed. It did not snap or break, but seemed rather to crumble to pieces, like dust, covering him with a fine white powder. The dull noise of its fall had echoed to silence before anyone spoke.

"That's odd," said the Professor, half to himself, "very odd. Ever see anything like that, Biggleswort h?" he added, turning to the pilot.

Biggles and Algy joined him on the bank, leaving Smyth in charge of the machine.

Algy picked up a stick of dead wood and crumbled it to

dust between his fingers. "There's something wrong about this place," he said again.

"What do you make of it?" asked the Professor in a low, strained voice, for the fall of the trees seemed to have damped his enthusiasm.

"I don't know," answered Biggles. "There seems to be a kind of plague about. It's foul; you can smell it. I can smell something else, too—a sort of scent—get it in whiffs. Heck! Smell that!"

For a second the air was heavy with perfume, then suddenly it died away again. It was as if the door of a perfumer's had been flung open and then shut. The scent was gloriously, wonderfully fragrant, with a heavy, sickly, and almost overpowering "end" to it.

"Come on!" cried the Professor. "Let's find out what it is," and he started off into the forest. He stopped and pointed at something on the ground. It was a skeleton, horribly human, about the size of a baby. "Monkey," he said laconically, and passed on.

They had walked for perhaps five minutes, still getting occasional whiffs of the perfume, when Algy stopped and mopped his face with a handkerchief.

Biggles looked back over his shoulder. "What's the matter?" he said. "You look ill."

"I feel darn sick," answered Algy shortly.

"Funny," said Biggles; "so do I. I believe this stink is getting in my stomach; it seems to be getting stronger, too."

The Professor, who had gone on ahead, pulled up dead in his tracks and stood staring at something straight ahead.

"Biggleswoth," he shouted, "hurry up—come and look at this!"

Biggles caught up with him and stopped in turn, staring, his lips parted in surprise. Straight ahead was a belt of undergrowth; there was nothing surprising in that, but it was the colour that astonished him. It was of an inconceivably brilliant emerald-green, a poisonous green, so vivid that it seemed possible to reach out and touch it. It may have been that the colourless monotony around intensified it, but for the moment it held him spellbound.

"Well, here it is, whatever it is," grunted the Professor, starting forward, and his shrill shout of delight brought Biggles forward at a run, only to pull up dead and gasp in wonderment.

Inside the growth was a mass of orchids. He understood little of orchidaceae, but sufficient to know that nothing like it had ever been seen before. The actual flowers were more like cypripediums than any other, except that near the ground there were masses of pseudo-bulbs like those of the common ceologyne; but again it was the colour that shook him.

They were blue. The under sepal was a deep, glowing royal blue, watered into a brilliant peacock-blue at the tip. Two orange spots, like eyes, were set at the base, and a long scarlet stigma completed the most devilishly beautiful thing that ever grew on earth. They were the size of dinner plates—and there were hundreds of them—thousands of them. They sprawled over the ground and piled up in great banks. They projected in long sprays from the trunks of the trees and hung in azure cascades from the branches over their heads. It may have been imagination, but it struck Biggles that all the flowers were facing his direction, as if they were looking at him. He glanced at Smilee.

The Professor's face was as pale as death and his lips were twitching curiously. He reached out his hand and plucked one of the flowers, but a sharp "ugh!" broke from his lips as he did so and he dropped it with a violent shudder, as a child drops an insect placed unexpectedly in its hand.

"It moved!" he gasped. "Bigglesworth, I swear it moved—look at it!" His voice rose to a shrill falsetto, and Biggles stared with loathing and horror at the thing at his feet, for it was twisting and turning like a piece of gelatine on a moist surface.

Suddenly the air was filled with an overpowering flood of perfume, and Biggles staggered back with a hoarse cry, clutching at his throat, a grim suspicion forming in his mind.

"Come on, Smilee!" he cried. "It's poison—run for it!"

He saw the Professor turn to run, but his feet caught in a tangled heap of the bulbs, and he fell headlong amongst the flowers. He staggered to his feet, making queer choking noises and, clutching wildly at the air, plunged blindly into an alley that led into the very heart of the growth.

"This way——" Biggles tried to shout, but the words were a croaking whisper. He felt his senses leaving him; the flowers spun dizzily before his eyes in a whirling band of blue. He could no longer see clearly, and turning, staggered, swaying from side to side, towards the lake. He clutched at a tree to save himself from falling, but it was as soft as cotton wool and came down with a "whoosh," smothering him with a cloud of rotting fibre. He rose, fighting to keep his reeling senses . . . vaguely he heard a voice shouting . . .

III

He opened his eyes drowsily as consciousness slowly returned, and for some minutes lay gazing unseeingly at a tangled confusion of branches passing in silent procession overhead. Presently he realized that his lips were dry and burning, that his head ached violently, and that he was going to be sick. With an effort he raised himself on to his elbow and looked blankly around him at his position.

He was lying half inside the cabin of the "Vandal", which was drifting slowly with the current down a broad river. Recollection of what had happened came back to him with a rush, and he crawled with difficulty into the cabin. The first thing he saw was Algy's face, blue-lipped, and grey with the pallor of death, in the pilot's seat. Smyth, face downwards, was sprawled across him. At first he thought they were both dead, but a closer examination revealed that they were both still breathing faintly. Ripping off his jacket he trailed it in the water for a moment, and then entered the cabin and held it over them. With difficulty he hauled the unconscious form of Smyth off Algy, and contrived to get the other into a sitting position in the seat.

Algy opened his eyes slowly and stared at him. "Water!"

he gasped, and Biggles wrung out the coat, allowing the drips to fall into the open mouth. Algy stirred and moved himself into a more comfortable position, still staring at his partner with wide-open eyes. "What was it?" he whispered.

"Hang on, laddie," said Biggles. "Let me see to Smyth."

In a few minutes he had brought him round, taxied to the bank, and moored the machine to a projecting root. He then made a pot of coffee, and the steaming liquid went far to restore them to normal, although they were all violently sick. Up to this time no one had mentioned the Professor.

"Where did he go?" asked Algy quietly at last.

Biggles shook his head. "Goodness knows," he said; "I don't. I don't even know how I got here."

"Neither do I," replied Algy. "I saw you staggering about as if you were crazy, and then you fell down. I remember running up and starting to drag you towards the lake, and that's all I know."

"I saw you dragging him," broke in Smyth, "and then you fell down too. I was being as sick as a dog, but I managed to haul you both to the machine and get you aboard. I just remember dropping Mr. Lacey into the pilot's seat and cutting the mooring rope, and then I must have packed up, too."

"Thanks, Smyth," said Biggles quietly. "We were both goners if you hadn't done that. Heck! That's how that collector—what was his name?—Hutson—went out. But the point is, where are we? We shall have to go back and look for the Professor."

They started the engine and taxied back upstream.

"The trouble is," said Biggles after a while, "we don't know how long we were unconscious, or which of these tributaries we came down. It might have been any one of those." He pointed to rivers on either bank which flowed into the main stream.

By evening they had failed to find the lake, and the pilot was getting worried about the petrol they were using.

"We can't go on like this," he observed. "If we find a long straight stretch of water I'm going to try and get her off; we shall be able to see where we are from the air, but frankly, I don't think it's much use looking for poor Smilee. We can't just leave him, though."

A fairly straight stretch of water, terminating in a cataract, came into view as they rounded the next bend, and Biggles eyed it grimly.

"Well," he said, "that settles it; we didn't come over that waterfall. We are on the Beni and we must have drifted in from one of those tributaries we passed. Goodness knows which one it was. It's getting dark; we'd better tie up while we can and get off again as soon as it is light."

The following morning Biggles taxied up as far as the cataract to make sure there were no obstructions on the water, and then roared down the stream, throttle wide open. There was a slight breeze in their favour and the "Vandal" came off the water without effort.

They saw the lake almost at once, and Algy pointed with outstretched finger. It lay a few miles to the left, but it was not that which made Biggles stare in stunned consternation.

"Were you smoking when you fell?" yelled Algy above the roar of the engine.

Biggles nodded.

"Your cigarette must have started the fire—the place was like tinder."

Again the pilot nodded and watched the scene below, where for miles a fire was raging over the area of the dead trees. Sparks were falling in showers into the lake. Great blackened areas, still smouldering, showed where the fire had already burnt itself out, or died as it came in contact with the living forest. A mighty cloud of smoke rose high into the air and billowed away across the tree-tops.

Biggles caught Algy's eye and shook his head; sadly he turned the nose of the machine towards the distant mountains.

CHAPTER 4

FAIR CARGO

"HELLO! What's all this?" Biggles looked in surprise at a formidable heap of letters on the table as he entered his room in the Hotel Guibert in La Paz. "It looks as if we are on the road to fame and fortune," he observed dryly to Algy, as he opened a letter at random. "Listen to this! Here's a fellow wants us to go and look for a ruined city in Yucatan."

"No, thank you; I saw quite enough of mangrove swamps on British Guiana," replied Algy quickly.

"How about this for a proposition? A Valparaiso hotel-keeper wants us to fetch cargoes of live lobsters from Juan Fernandez."

"Not for me," returned Algy incisively. "They might get loose; I've no desire to be torn to pieces in mid-air by infuriated crustaceans."

"What's this one? How about doing anti-poacher patrols of the guano islands for the Chilean Government?"

"Definitely, no; guano is too unromantic; besides, it smells."

"Would you like to go spotting for the eyrie of a king-condor for a film company? They offer five thousand dollars."

"That sounds more interesting. Anything else?"

"Yes. Good heavens! Here's a letter from Sandy Wyndham. You remember Sandy of 207 Squadron—he fell off the wind-stocking pole the day he got that Heinkel over Hamel, and broke both his legs. He went home and I haven't heard of him since. Listen to this.

"Dear Biggles,

"I have just been reading about your affair in Bolivia; it's in the home papers. Good show. Do you want to pick up an easy packet of money? I am in the coconut business now, and have a plantation at Rarotayo, one of the Tonga group of islands. I am home on leave at present, but shall be returning via Panama, arriving there on December 4th. Will you meet me there, as, if so, I will get off and go on by the next boat. Radio-telegraph reply as I shall be at sea when you get this. I am sailing on the s.s. 'Antinous'. Cheerios to Algy. All the best.

"Sandy."

"What do you make of that?" asked Biggles, looking up.

"It's no use sitting here guessing. Let's go and meet him, by all means. Sandy has done enough flying to know what he's talking about. If we are going we've no time to lose."

"All right; tell Smyth to get the machine ready; we'll start in the morning."

II

Biggles leaned pensively against the somewhat flimsy rail that surrounded the *patio* of the low adobe rest-house which snuggled amid a tangle of cactus and palm near the sun-baked aerodrome at Buenaventura, where the crew of the "Vandal" had perforce broken their long journey to Panama.

The night air was still, and fragrant with the scent of night-flowering cacti that lifted their waxen petals to the tropic moon, and the bougainvillæa that clambered untidily up the stone pillars which supported the long, overhanging eaves of the pantiled roof.

Biggles yawned and turned slowly to where Algy reclined in a long cane chair near a feeble oil-lamp, a newspaper dangling between his fingers.

"Still pining for Consuelo?" he bantered.

"As a matter of fact," replied Algy coldly, "I was just thinking what a good thing it was we didn't roll up here a few days ago, or the 'Vandal' might have been commandeered. It seems that Colombia has been writhing in the throes of one of its periodical revolutions, but it's all over now. The rebels have been badly bent, or, rather, busted, and the President's O.C. troops, Generalissimo Pedro da Alligante, is now pursuing the popular pastime of reducing the survivors to produce* by the simple expedient of lining them up against a wall and mowing them down with a machine-gun."

"Nice feller."

"Charming. It seems that he's peeved because the leader of the insurrection, young José Oliviera, has so far escaped his blood-stained vengeance."

"I can't understand why people have to squabble in a

* *Service expression, meaning "broken up".*

country like this," observed Biggles disinterestedly, turning once more to the contemplation of the black yet soft lattice-work shadows of the palms.

"Bah! If *you* lived here you'd have half a dozen revolutions running at the same time," sneered Algy, "but what about a spot of shut-eye, it's getting latish—hello——"

He sprang to his feet in puzzled astonishment, as a girl, dressed in a dark clinging gown, with the inevitable mantilla draped around her shoulders, ran swiftly up the steps from the shadows and stood panting before them, her breast rising and falling spasmodically from exertion or agitation, her southern beauty in no way marred by the tears that hung on the lashes of her dark, appealing eyes, now turning from one to the other in tremulous hesitation. Then, with a swift Latin gesture she turned to Biggles and held out her hands.

"*Señor,*" she faltered.

"Gently, lady, gently," muttered Biggles uncomfortably, as the girl's body shook with a convulsive, uncontrollable sob, and then, turning to Algy, "Come and do your stuff, laddie; this is more in your line."

Algy needed no second invitation. "*Que tiente va, señorita?*" he asked anxiously, in his best Spanish.

"Tomorrow I am to be married," cried the girl in tones of anguish.

"Why weep about it?" said Biggles, raising his eyebrows.

"My father has given me to the hateful——" she looked around furtively—"Don Pedro da Alligante. But I will not; I will die by my own hand first," she whispered fiercely.

"Oh, don't do that," replied Biggles awkwardly. "What can *we* do about it, anyway?"

"Help me to escape, *señor*—take me with you——"

"You shall come with me, *señorita*," declared Algy. "I——"

"Not so fast, laddie, not so fast," broke in Biggles, and then to the girl: "Why not run away? I mean, there are horses and railways and things?"

"They would catch me, only you can save me——"

"But you don't know where we're going!"

"It matters not—anywhere——"

"But what is Don Pedro going to say when he discovers I have run away with his beautiful bride?" protested Biggles. "We don't want to be involved in trouble with——"

"Rot!" snapped Algy. "Let the girl come if she wants to; no one's likely to know, anyway." He turned to the girl. "We are going to Panama; we may land at Cristobal."

"I have friends in Cristobal who will protect me!" cried the girl eagerly.

Biggles shrugged his shoulders. "All right," he said slowly, "but for heaven's sake keep quiet about it. I don't want to get tangled up with domestic affairs——"

"Domestic my eye!' snorted Algy. "You can't throw the girl into the blood-stained paws of that——"

"Careful," warned Biggles, glancing around, and then to the girl, "You run along now, *señorita*. Look, there is our aeroplane, over there," he went on, pointing to the amphibian. "You hide yourself in the cabin and then we shall know nothing about it, *sabe?* By the way, I didn't catch your name."

"Juanita."

"All right, Juanita; you trot along and do as you're told."

The girl nodded, her lips parted with eagerness and gratitude. "*Gracias, señor, gracias*; I will do anything——"

"Yes, I know," interrupted Biggles coldly, "but you go along and get some more clothes on; we start early in the morning and it may be cold."

The girl seized his hand, pressed it to her lips, and then, turning, vanished into the shadows whence she came.

III

The sky became pale and lifeless as the moon's silver gleam grew dim in a pallid twilight. It was five o'clock, and the sun, on its upward course, stabbed its first flickering beam into the heavens as Biggles, with Algy at his side, crossed over to the amphibian standing in the shade of the Pan-American Airways hangar, and nodded to Smyth, their mechanic, who was standing by the engine.

"Everything all right?" he asked shortly.

"O.K., sir," was the crisp reply.

"Has—er—anyone arrived?"

Smyth, with the pardonable familiarity of long service, flickered his eyelid and jabbed his thumb in the direction of the cabin. "She's inside, sir," he murmured out of the corner of his mouth.

Biggles climbed into the cabin, followed by Algy and Smyth.

The engine split the silence with its powerful bellow,

which faded away to a rhythmic murmur as the pilot throttled back to allow it to warm up. For five minutes they sat thus. The aerodrome was deserted except for a couple of American mechanics who stood by the door of their hangar watching the "Vandal" curiously. Then, from the distance, came the sound of voices, shouting. Biggles turned his head casually in the direction of the sound, and stiffened into an attitude of tense expectancy as his eye fell on a troop of cavalry, led by an officer, galloping towards them.

"The troops are on parade early," observed Algy, with interest.

"Yes; I should say it's our friend of the blood-stained hands, looking for his little sweetheart," replied Biggles sternly. "We'd better be moving or we may find ourselves in one of his shooting parties." He thrust the throttle open in a series of jerks that swung the "Vandal" round in its own length, and then swept across the sun-scorched aerodrome, leaving a swirling trail of dust in his wake.

At a thousand feet they circled and looked down. The soldiers had reined in their horses and were staring upwards; the officer was shaking his drawn sabre.

"Look; he's waving us goodbye," grinned Algy.

Five hours later the "Vandal" ran to a bumpy standstill on the aerodrome at Cristobal. Slowly the pilot taxied along the boundary hedge of prickly pear to the offices of the American Air Line Company, and then turned to the low door leading to the cabin.

"Picture of a knight-errant collecting ransom," jeered Algy.

"Don't be coarse," returned Biggles reproachfully. "Hello; where's the lady, Smyth?"

"She's gone, sir."

"Gone!"

"Yes, she opened the door and stepped out while you were taxi-ing in and hurried off round the back there somewhere."

"Well, I'm blowed! Women for gratitude!" He grinned as he saw Algy's crestfallen face looking in the cabin door.

"Fancy her pushing off like that without so much as a *gracias*," muttered Algy bitterly.

"What else did you expect?" asked Biggles.

Algy eyed him coldly, but said nothing.

"Never mind," laughed Biggles; "come and have a drink—something less intoxicating than Spanish *señoritas*."

They were still puzzled about Juanita when, an hour later, a north-bound Pan-American plane landed and taxied up to discharge its passengers. As the door opened and the first passenger alighted Biggles dropped the glass he was holding with a crash, his jaw sagging foolishly. It was Juanita.

At the same moment a handsome olive-complexioned young man detached himself from the small group of spectators and hurried to meet her. Regardless of the stares and smiles of the onlookers they flung their arms about each other in a fervent embrace; words of endearment, in liquid Spanish, floated to the ears of the two pilots. Slowly, with eyes for no one but themselves, the lovers walked towards the exit; as they drew abreast of the spellbound pilots, a rose that the girl wore on her gown became detached and fell to the ground. Biggles watched them disappear round the corner before he stooped and picked it up.

"Tell me," he asked the pilot of the plane, who had just entered, "who are they?"

"Those two? That's the famous *señora* Juanita Oliviera and young Don José, her husband, though how he got up here I don't know. He was mixed up in that last revolution in Colombia and they're searching for him high and low down there. Smart dame, isn't she?"

"Yes—she is," replied Biggles absently, with a curious smile, as he dropped the rose in his pocket.

CHAPTER 5

BEAUTY AND THE BEAST

"YOU'LL probably think I'm crazy," said Sandy, after greetings had been exchanged and they had settled themselves on the veranda of the Baltimore Hotel in Panama, and with iced drinks before them prepared to listen to Sandy's tale.

"In the first place I had better tell you that after leaving the Service I went to Malaya, rubber-planting. Things went wrong and I drifted about until I got a job at one of the trading posts of the North Equatorial Company. I made a bit of money in copra and shell, and a couple of years ago started off on my own. I now have a nice little place at Rarotayo.

"About eighteen months ago I happened to mention pearls to my head boy, who, by the way, is a real old Polynesian. He told me quite casually that he knew where there were plenty, but it was impossible to get them. You may be sure I wasn't long asking him where they were. He told me they were at the Kaisiora; that made me laugh, and I'll tell you why. The Kaisiora is a big circular reef about forty miles from my place. It's an almost perfect atoll. Try and imagine an island about three miles long and a mile wide, and not more than four or five feet high at the highest place. As a matter of fact, you can't see the island because the rollers sweep right over it, or appear to. All you can see, even on a calm day, is a great white patch of boiling surf nearly hidden under a cloud of spray; you can hear the boom of the breakers miles away. In short, it is a thing to give a sailor the horrors, and I don't suppose a ship has been near it in years. Actually the place is shown on the chart as British, but goodness knows why, as it is quite certain nobody ever landed there.

"Well, this is the story Tauri—that's the name of my boy—told me. I've been good to him, and I believe he was telling the truth. Many years ago, when he was a young man, he set out from Tahiti as one of the crew of a big war-canoe. The old Polynesians used to travel hundreds of miles in them. They got caught in a typhoon and were driven into the Kaisiora, and he meant it literally. The island isn't an island in the real sense of the word. He says it is a huge oval-shaped coral reef, or atoll, with a perfectly calm lagoon in the middle. Apparently, by an amazing stroke of luck, the canoe was picked up bodily by a comber and thrown clean over the top of the reef into the lagoon. A tremendous sea was running, and I must say that it does not seem impossible. Inside they were sheltered from the wind and were able to ride out the storm. When the wind went down they looked for a way out. There was no way. They were penned up inside. On all sides huge seas pounded up over rows of jagged coral teeth. They sat there for a month, living on shell fish from the floor of the lagoon, which is quite shallow, not more than thirty feet deep, but shelving down into a deep hole at one end. It sounds rather as if the place was the crater of an extinct volcano. Now you begin to get the hang of things."

He paused dramatically to light a fresh cigarette.

"The floor of the lagoon is a solid bed of shell, untouched, the sort of thing pearlers dream about, but never find. The oysters get thrown in and they can't get out, and that's been going on for I don't know how many years. Just imagine it! Well, they're there for the getting.

"Ultimately the crew of the war-canoe tried to get out. Twenty-four out of twenty-eight were drowned in the surf; the other four found themselves outside, hanging on to a broken, capsized canoe, with no paddles. Sharks got two of them; one went crazy. Tauri was picked up by a schooner and the skipper put him before the mast and beat hell out of him before he could get away. He told me he had quite a number of splendid pearls, but lost them in the struggle getting out of the lagoon.

"Well, I've got a motor-boat, and when Tauri pitched me this yarn I couldn't get to the Kaisiora fast enough. I had decided that if there was a fortune in pearls waiting to be picked up nothing would keep me out, but I was wrong. There is no break in the reef, and no one but a madman would try and get through the surf. I nearly went mad trying to work out how to get inside, yet, strangely enough, I never thought of an aeroplane till I read about your show in Bolivia, and then it struck me like an inspiration that with a flying-boat, or an amphibian like yours, the thing was simplicity itself."

"How do you suggest we should go to work?" interrupted Biggles.

"I suggest that you ship your machine to Raratonga by the next boat, which I shall have to go on, anyway. From there we can fly to my place. Using my own lagoon as a base, all we have to do is to fly to the Kaisiora, land on the lagoon, load up with shell and bring it back. Tauri will do the diving. We can keep that up till we've cleared the whole bed. My boat can patrol between the islands and pick us up, or tow the machine in, if we have a forced landing," he concluded enthusiastically.

"It sounds pretty good to me," acknowledged Biggles. "How about you, Algy?"

"Let's see about getting the wings off the 'Vandal'," was the quick reply; "that's all that should be necessary. We can ship her as deck-cargo, I should think."

II

The "Vandal", her engine purring sweetly, sat on the quiet water of Sandy's lagoon at Rarotayo, ready for the first trip to the Kaisiora. The weather was perfect for the expedition, and the early-morning sunshine poured down from a sky of cloudless blue on to the little group outside a palm-thatched bungalow on the beach, near to where the "Vandal" was moored. A pyramid of red-painted petrol-cans, just delivered by a trading schooner, made a vivid spot of colour against the deep shade of the plantation behind.

The three white men were dressed only in shorts, shirts,

and canvas shoes, for the weather was warm. Tauri, who was accompanying the expedition as a diver, was clad only in a thick layer of coconut oil, under which his brown skin gleamed like satin. Smyth, the mechanic, had been given charge of the motor-boat which was to patrol the intervening stretch of water.

Their only equipment was a large stone attached to a rope, and a basket to raise the shell to the surface. At the last moment Sandy picked up a small axe.

"We had better take this in case Tauri gets anchored to the bottom by a big clam," he observed. "They are more dangerous to divers than sharks," he added, throwing the instrument aboard, little dreaming that within the next few hours it was to be the means of saving all their lives.

They took their places in the machine, and the pilot taxied into position for the take-off. The engine roared as he opened the throttle, and a moment later the island, with its palm-fringed beach of coral sand, lay below. They circled for a few minutes, climbing for height, and then headed out over the open sea on a compass course to their destination, which, in the crystal-clear atmosphere, was soon visible ahead.

Twice the pilot circled low over the steaming reef, examining the lagoon closely for rocks or other obstructions which might damage the fragile hull of the amphibian. Seen from the air it presented an extraordinary appearance, and it was at once obvious that Tauri had spoken the truth, at least as far as his description of the place was concerned.

Set in a sea of the deepest ultramarine was an almost perfect oval of snow-white surf through which the jagged coral here and there showed its teeth. Within it was the still, emerald-green lagoon, shading down to a deeper green and finally merging into purple-black at one end. Like an emerald set in diamonds on a velvet robe, thought the pilot, as he throttled back and glided on to the perfect anchorage. The "Vandal" finished its run as the pilot switched off, and floated motionless on the green water, while the airmen stood lost in wonderment at the exquisite beauty of the scene around them. They were in the centre of one of Nature's masterpieces.

Every colour of the artist's palette was represented, each one a patch of brilliancy, but the whole blending, as though seen through the ground-glass screen of a camera out of focus, into tones of unimaginable softness, and forms of incomparable loveliness. Deep violet roots of coral thrust long, delicate rose-pink antennae into the sun-soaked spray. Cones of pale blue and mauve lifted themselves into curious regular groups from symmetrical, amethyst-tinted, sponge-like foundations beneath a cream and lemon tracery of inconceivable delicacy. Fans of old gold and ivory, some open, some closed, stood side by side with jewel-encrusted combs more beautiful than those of old Madrid.

It was hard to see where the coral ended and the floor of the lagoon began; of ethereal purity and as transparent as the air about them, the water was only visible where it lapped gently against the hull of the machine. Beneath them, fish of incredible colours and unbelievable designs, singly, and in little shoals, floated, seemingly in space, aimlessly, and with effortless ease.

"Great Scott!" The words, spoken in an awe-stricken whisper, came from Sandy, who, with parted lips, was staring downwards. His face was pale and the hands that rested lightly on the edge of the cockpit were trembling. "Look!" he said in an unnatural high-pitched voice, and then burst into a peal of hysterical laughter. Biggles, looking eagerly below, could see ghostly luminous white spots shining on the floor of the lagoon.

"What is it?" he asked

"Shell—tons of it," replied Sandy, recovering himself with an effort.

"You mean they're oysters—open, down there?"

But Sandy was not listening. He had the weighted line over the side in an instant. Tauri, goggled, his teeth flashing a broad smile of eagerness, had seized the rope with one hand and the prehensile toes of one foot and was dropping with the stone into the depths.

The watchers on the boat could see every movement distinctly, how he tore the molluscs from their hold and piled them into the basket. He shot up to the surface for air; the basket was emptied in the cabin, and he plunged down again. For half an hour he worked steadily, and by that time they had as heavy a load of shell as they dared risk carrying.

"We'll get this home and come back for more," declared Biggles, winding the self-starter.

"Take it quietly," Sandy told him, leaning over the side of the hull. "Taxi slowly down to the far end; we might as well see how far the shell-bed stretches . . . Tauri was right; it gets deeper here," he shouted a few moments later.

Algy, leaning over the other side, gazed with interest at the quickly shelving floor of the lagoon. The colour of the water became more intense and then he could no longer see the bottom. He had a slight twinge of vertigo as he stared into the unfathomable depths. It was as if the machine hung poised in space on the edge of a precipice, with a pale-blue infinity above and a deep-blue void below. He noticed several fish darting swiftly away and was about to turn when another movement caught his eye.

At first it seemed as if the bottom of the sea was slowly rising to meet them—not *all* the bottom, but a large circular part of it. It seemed to be bringing two enormous open oyster-shells with it, two discs of dully-smouldering opalescent white.

It was not until a thick snake-like coil detached itself from the bulk and groped feelingly upwards that he realized he was looking at an octopus, a monstrous horror of the deep, far exceeding in size anything he had ever imagined. For a moment he stared spell-bound, stunned into tongue-tied silence . . . and then he screamed.

Biggles, after one glance at the ashen face beside him, had thrust the throttle wide open and kicked the rudder-bar full over to swing round into the wind. But he was too late. The machine gave a wild lurch and remained motionless, the nose cocked high into the air as the tail was drawn down. Glancing over his shoulder, the pilot saw something like a thick rope curled over the end of the fuselage just in front of the tailplanes. A great weight had already dragged half the tail-unit under water.

In the nightmare-like horror of the next few seconds things seemed to happen with a slow deliberation that was appalling, and with such vivid clarity that no detail escaped him. All fear seemed to vanish in the pent-up intensity of the moment, and he watched with the fascination of a spectator. Such movements as he made were purely instinctive.

He saw Tauri spring up out of the cabin, axe in hand, and then run swiftly down the fuselage towards the tail. The axe flashed in the sunlight, swept over and down, sheared through the mighty tentacle and sank with a thud into the woodwork of the hull, where it remained quivering. The tail, released from its ghastly anchor, instantly leapt upwards and sideways. Tauri, thrown off his balance, made a desperate leap for the leading edge of the tailplane, missed it, and disappeared from sight. The machine, churning up a sea of foam, swung round in its own length and leapt forward under the full power of the engine. Tauri came into view, swimming as only an islander can swim; his brown arms flashed through the air like twin propellers and his legs pounded the water like pistons as he raced towards the reef. Behind him surged a great ripple; under it was a broad black shadow.

The pilot throttled back a trifle and touched the rudder-bar lightly to bring the machine in line with pursuer and pursued. As he neared them he swung round the ripple in a wild swerve and bore down upon the swimming native. Out of the corner of his eye he saw a great tentacle break the surface and grope horribly towards his wing-tip, but his eyes were fixed on the man in front, now within thirty yards of the reef. "Catch him!" he yelled.

Algy leaned far over the side, arms outstretched to grasp the gasping Polynesian. Ten yards—five—their hands met. Just what happened after he took the man's weight and pulled, he never knew. Whether it was the speed of the machine, he was unable to say, but the next second he was in the water, striking out madly towards the reef.

Biggles made a frantic grab at his feet as he disappeared overboard, but missed him. Behind him, the waving tentacles were within twenty yards. In front was the reef, and there was not room to turn. He thrust the throttle wide open and jerked the joystick back into his stomach. The machine lifted off the water, wobbled for a moment at stalling speed, and then, almost grazing the top of the reef, picked up and soared into the air. Swinging round in a desperate climbing turn, he could take in the whole situation at a glance.

Algy and Tauri had reached the reef and were scrambling wildly for the highest point. The octopus, looking like a great bloated spider, lay about fifty yards away in the shallow part of the lagoon. The pilot watched the two men on the reef crawl down the far side and crouch beneath the flying spray of the ocean rollers. Twice he glided down towards the lagoon as if to land, but each time the giant octopus moved sideways towards him and he knew that it was watching him. Landing was obviously out of the question. Suddenly he swung round and headed away over the open sea towards Rarotayo.

III

Although Algy knew that Biggles would not have left him unless he had a definite plan in his mind, he watched the machine disappear into the blue distance with consternation.

"We finish altogether, eh, boss?" observed the Tahitian calmly, at last.

"Finish nothing," replied Algy shortly, with a conviction he was far from feeling.

"Big fella him kai-kai us plenty," murmured Tauri philosophically.

"That fella no walk on rocks, eh?" asked Algy in dismay.

"Him walk pretty quick," answered Tauri grimly.

Algy did not reply, but lying on his stomach peered through a tracery of coral to where the monster lay like a dark stain on the water, the stump of its severed tentacle waving gently above the surface.

He wondered how Biggles hoped to cope with the horror. There was no point in fetching the boat to their assistance, for between them and the open sea was fifty yards of creamy foam where the ocean rollers pounded with a force sufficient to smash a boat or a human being to pulp in a moment of time. Whatever was to be done would have to be done before nightfall, for after a night spent on the reef among the crawling horrors, which he knew would come out after dark, dawn would probably find them gibbering lunatics.

An hour passed slowly. Several sea-birds had arrived

and were circling round them, uttering plaintive cries. For some minutes Algy watched them disinterestedly, and then, with a sudden horrible suspicion in his mind, he crawled to the top of the reef and peeped over. One glance and his worst fears were realized. With a slow, half-crawling half-rolling motion, the octopus was coming in their direction, attracted no doubt by the actions of the birds.

"We finish together," observed Tauri with pathetic fatalism.

For a few moments Algy came near to panic, and looked at the foaming surf as if considering plunging headlong in. Then a distant sound caught his ear and he listened tensely.

"Other boss he come plenty quick," said Tauri hopefully, pointing to a distant but rapidly approaching speck in the sky.

But the horror was approaching too, with ghastly deliberation. With one accord the two men crawled down as near to the breakers as they dared, and started to work their way along the reef. Progress was slow, for the coral was slippery and razor-sharp in places. Looking back, they saw the monster crawling up on the reef where they had been a few moments before, but the "Vandal" was roaring overhead now, and the monster stopped, evidently in order to look at it.

Algy anxiously watched the machine for a signal. He saw Sandy wave as the pilot banked; then the machine flattened out and raced straight along the reef, passing so close that he could almost touch it. As it roared over the octopus a bulky object hurled downwards and the machine zoomed high.

Algy was unprepared for what followed. A sheet of flame leapt upwards; there was a thundering detonation that shook the reef and the air was full of flying coral. He was flung down heavily by the force of the explosion. He covered his head with his arms until the rain of coral had ceased, and then he rose to his feet and looked towards the place where the octopus had been. A great hole yawned in the coral, but the octopus was swimming strongly towards the deep end of the lagoon. Again the "Vandal" swooped low, and then zoomed high. A column of water sprang skywards and the surface of the lagoon was churned into foam.

The amphibian glided in, and without waiting to finish its run, taxied swiftly towards them.

"Come on!" yelled the pilot from the cockpit.

They needed no second invitation. Plunging into the water, they reached the machine in a few strokes and hauled themselves aboard. The engine roared as the pilot opened the throttle, and they soared upwards into the blue.

IV

"That's a nice little lot," observed Sandy a few days later as they sat around a table in his bungalow. The objects of their attention lay on a small piece of cloth; they were pearls—seven fine pearls and a number of smaller ones, known as seed-pearls. "Just think what that lagoon must be worth," he mused. "What a pity I couldn't hit that monster; but I didn't, and there it is. I damaged it, but it managed to get back into its hole. It may be dead now, but I'm dashed if I feel like risking it. Tauri wouldn't dive there again, anyway," he added.

"And I wouldn't land there again," observed Algy emphatically. "It was a bit of luck you had those few sticks of dynamite, or I don't like to think where I should have been by now!" he concluded soberly.

CHAPTER 6

BOB'S BOX

THE FOUR white men on the beach at Rarotayo watched the trim, white-painted schooner feel her way carefully through the opening in the reef and drop her anchor with a splash in the blue, crystal-clear water of the lagoon near to where the "Vandal" swung gently at her moorings.

"It's the *Sea Eagle*, Sven Ericson's schooner," announced Sandy to Biggles. "It's about his time. He's a good old scout, one of the old-timers, who has spent his life in the Islands. Plenty of money, always going home, but can't tear himself away. You'll like him. Well, here he comes," he went on, as a boat was lowered and rowed vigorously towards them by two stalwart natives. "You'll have to stay and meet him if only to hear the latest gossip."

"We're in no hurry," observed Biggles; "tomorrow will suit us as well as today, provided the weather holds; but if I don't soon make an effort I shall never go."

A month had passed since the affair at Kaisiora, and the crew of the "Vandal" were ready to leave for Australia, where they proposed to sell the machine, or, failing that, have her thoroughly overhauled and then fly her back to England.

"Ahoy there, Sandy!" yelled the captain of the schooner jovially, jumping into the shallow water and wading ashore. "Quite a crowd, eh? Time old fellows like me went home when the Islands come to this"—he jerked his thumb ruefully towards the aircraft. "Heck! What would they have said in the old days?"

"Never mind the old days; come and have a drink," laughed Sandy, leading the way to the bungalow.

"So! You fly the aeroplane, eh?" observed Ericson, looking Biggles up and down curiously. "I've often wondered what aviators looked like. For me, I stay on the water, where I can see what is underneath," he concluded firmly, picking up his drink.

Biggles looked at the weather-beaten face of the giant red-headed Swede, and smiled. "I can see what is beneath better than you can," he told him.

"Eh? What's that? You can see better than I can from the deck of my schooner? How so?"

"From the air I can see right through the water to the bottom of the sea—unless it is very deep," replied Biggles.

Ericson looked at him incredulously.

"He's quite right, Skipper," broke in Sandy. "Didn't you know that during the war they used aeroplanes for spotting submarines on the bottom?"

The Swede drew in his breath with a low whistle of surprise. "Why didn't I know that before?" he muttered half to himself.

He was very quiet during lunch. Once or twice Biggles saw him look up as if about to speak, but each time he changed his mind and frowned, as though wrestling with a difficult problem. Immediately after the meal was finished he took Sandy on one side and spoke to him in an undertone.

"Ask him yourself," replied Sandy loudly, with a wink at Biggles, as they settled down in the cane chairs on the veranda.

Ericson looked at the pilot anxiously. "Are you open to consider a proposition—a business proposition?" he asked, a trifle apologetically.

"Certainly," replied Biggles. "We'll tackle anything within reason; what is it?"

"You'd better tell him the whole story, Skipper," said Sandy, turning to Ericson. "He'll get the hang of the thing then."

The Swede cut some tobacco off a roll with a clasp-knife, rolled it between his horny palms, and filled his pipe with slow deliberation.

"Did you ever hear of Robert McKane?" he asked, sending a cloud of pungent blue smoke into the still air.

"Never," replied Biggles briefly.

"No? I don't suppose you would," went on the other, "but you'd have known about him if you'd lived in these parts a few years ago. Big Bob we called him. Well, Bob drifted into the Islands just after I did, and that'd be nearly forty years ago; things were different then. McKane wasn't his real name, of course, but that doesn't matter down here; we call a man by the name he chooses down here, and that isn't always the one he was christened. There was some as said that Bob had been an officer in the British Navy and got chucked out for something or other; others said his wife went off the rails and drove him *moost*. That's as maybe. He had a handle to his real name, though, and I happen to know that because"—the Skipper paused reflectively—"but what does it matter?

"Bob and his schooner, the *Southern Star*," he continued, "were soon known from Singapore to Thursday Island. He took on anything that came along, and what with blackbirding, copra, and shell, he must have piled up a tidy bit of money. He kept it in his cabin; at least, his boys used to talk about the box he had there which he was always popping down to look at, but nobody ever saw what was inside it.

"It would be about November, 'thirty-five, when he tore the bottom off the *Southern Star* on an uncharted reef near Gospel Island; I never pass the place now without thinking about him. He turned up at Port Moresby in a native prahu about a month later and he was never the same man afterwards. He had lost his box. Everybody knew about it, of course, and he had plenty of offers to help, but he wouldn't take 'em, apparently because he didn't like parting with any share of his boodle.

"It took him a year or two to get enough money together to get another schooner with diving equipment; as a matter of fact, he bought an old junk, which he re-named the *Lisbeth*, off a Chink trader at Moresby, and off he went to look for the *Southern Star*. He spent about two years looking, and at the finish he had to put to sea with half a crew. He was so cantankerous that no one would sail with him.

"He lost the *Lisbeth* in the big blow in the autumn of nineteen-thirty-eight. Two years later he was still looking for the *Southern Star*, and tales began to be told about the size of his treasure. First it was a bag of pearls the size of pigeons' eggs; then it was the map of a lost gold-mine in the Solomons, and then it was the whereabouts of an old pirate-junk loaded with loot—goodness knows what wasn't in that box at the finish. 'Has Bob got his box yet?' became a sort of byword, and, 'When Bob gets his box' meant never.

"The war made no difference to Bob; he still went on looking. He was still looking when an enemy ship sent him to Davy Jones. One of his Solomon boys was taken off Gospel about six months later, and he reckoned he was the only survivor. When the news got out that Bob had gone there was a general rush to Gospel, and I joined it. I spent six months looking for the *Southern Star*, and so did a lot of others, but it was no go. The trouble was no one could say to within a mile or two where she went down; it was a dark night and there was a big sea running, and she drifted a bit before she settled down. The water isn't all that deep; in fact, it isn't more than ten or a dozen fathoms in most places, and that must have made Bob think he ought to find her. But he didn't; neither did anybody else. Now you understand why what you said to me just now about seeing through the water to the bottom made me think. If the *Southern Star* is there, and we know she is there, you wouldn't be long picking up her bearings."

Biggles nodded. "You're right," he agreed. "We

could cover fifty square miles while a diver was covering fifty yards."

"Well, if you'll find the wreck, I'll get the box up," offered Ericson. "I've got the latest diving equipment and a good diver. If you like the idea, I'll tell you what I'll do. I'll take my schooner to Gospel with plenty of stores; there is a good lagoon there, like this one, for you to land on. You find the wreck, I'll get the box, and we'll split the profit. How's that?"

"Suits me," replied Biggles. "How long will it take you to get to Gospel? We shall have to run down to Australia first for a complete overhaul, and you may have to cache petrol for me at one of the intermediate islands if Gospel is outside my range, but we can settle that later. Suppose we say we'll meet six weeks from today at Gospel? That will give us both plenty of time."

"Do me fine," agreed the Swede.

"I'm positively aching to know what's inside that box," declared Algy.

II

The airmen leaned over the rail of the *Sea Eagle* watching the diving operations with interest.

Their plans had worked out well. After a badly needed overhaul they had flown the "Vandal" to Gospel Island without incident or delay, and had arrived at the rendezvous a day before the appointed time. They had located the *Southern Star* on their second trip. The ill-fated schooner was lying some miles south of the reef that had sent her to the bottom, which probably explained why the others had failed to discover her. They had marked the spot by dropping a buoy, and all that remained to be done was for Ericson to fulfil his part of the bargain. His schooner had been quickly brought to the place, the diver had gone over the side, and the entire crew awaited developments with intense interest. Hardly a ripple disturbed the surface of the ocean; in fact, it was so calm that Biggles had landed the "Vandal" on the open sea near the schooner, to which it was now moored.

"I shall be thrilled to death to see what is inside that box," murmured Algy, as they watched the line of bubbles rising to the surface, showing where the diver was at work.

"So shall I, after the talk there has been for all these years," admitted Ericson. "Whatever it is it must be pretty valuable for a man like Bob to spend half his life looking for it. Hello, yes?" he called suddenly into the telephone he was holding, and then to the others, "He's got it," he announced in a voice which he strove to keep calm.

They had to curb their impatience for nearly half an hour before the diver, with a small barnacle-encrusted chest clasped in his arms, broke the surface and was lifted aboard. Ericson seized the chest, giving a ringing cheer, which was taken up by the entire crew, and with the airmen at his heels hurried to the cabin, where he placed it on the table.

He examined the heavy padlock, rushed from the room, and reappeared a moment later with a hammer and cold chisel in his hands. "Stand clear!" he cried, and the airmen stepped back to avoid the swing of the hammer. Three blows and the lock snapped. The Swede lifted the lid and peered inside.

He took out a small leather bag, which jingled unmistakably as he untied the string and poured a stream of fifty or sixty golden sovereigns on to the table. "He didn't spend all his money looking for those," he mused.

He extracted another small bag and rolled twelve or fifteen good-sized pearls into his palm. "Nor for those," he muttered, with a puzzled air.

Next came an old newspaper.

"Nor for that," observed Biggles dryly, from the far side of the table where he was standing.

Ericson looked back into the box, lifted out a folded sheet of tissue-paper, and stared at something that lay under it. The airmen saw him blink, bend forward and stare again. An extraordinary expression crept over his face, leaving it oddly white. His jaw sagged foolishly and he sucked in his breath with a sudden gasp. He raised his eyes to the others and his lips formed the words, "The treasure," but no sound came.

"What——?" began Biggles, but a shrill cry of alarm on deck cut him short. A babble of voices broke out, a medley of sounds in which one word stood out clearly.

Ericson jumped as if he had been shot and darted to the barometer. "The bottom's dropped out!" he gasped and sprang for the companionway. He reached the deck with Algy at his heels and yelled a volley of orders. Pandemonium had broken loose.

Algy took one glance upwards and swung round to look for Biggles. "Come on!" he cried shrilly. He heard the lid of the box slam below, and then Biggles bounded up the steps and joined him. On his face was an expression that Algy had never seen there before.

"What was in the——?"

"Get aboard your boat if you're going, but you had better cut it adrift and stay with me," roared Ericson. "I've slipped my cable. It'll hit us within five minutes."

Biggles looked around. The sun was no longer shining, but glowed in the sky like a great amber-coloured globe. A mist obscured the horizon; above it, from the south-east, a broad indigo belt was racing across the sky towards them at incredible speed. A sinister oily calm lay on the water. "Great Scott!" he gasped, darting towards the stern, where the "Vandal" was moored. Smyth had already cast off, but was hanging on to the ship's painter. "Quick!" snapped Biggles, dropping into the cockpit.

Algy sprang in beside him. "What was in the box?" he yelled.

Biggles's reply was lost in the roar of the engine as it sprang to life. Without another glance at the schooner he thrust the throttle wide open, swung up into the rapidly thickening haze, and banked in a steep climbing turn towards the island five or six miles away. They were still two miles from the lagoon, and the black belt of the typhoon almost overhead, when he yelled, "Strap in!"

They were just in time. Something solid seemed to rise up under the machine and lift it bodily a thousand feet or more into the air at the speed of an express lift.

Then the invisible force seemed to be suddenly snatched away and they braced themselves against the sides of the cabin as the machine dropped like a stone over a colossal "bump".

Biggles knew that it was the first wave of compressed air, packed into fluid-like density by the pressure of the oncoming typhoon. He caught his breath as they struck the firm air at the bottom of the bump with a force that made the machine vibrate from propeller-bosses to tail-wheel. Again the machine quivered and soared vertically, forcing them down in their seats, as an inferno of wind struck it. The pilot thrust the control-column forward with both hands and raced towards the sheltered lagoon on the leeward side of the island.

Algy glanced below and saw that the sea had turned grey. There were no waves, but a raging wind was ripping the surface off the water in a smother of spray; it was like looking down on to the top of a bank of nimbus-cloud. There was no sign of the *Sea Eagle*.

A spatter of hailstones struck the machine like a burst of machine-gun bullets, and the pilot, knowing full well that hailstones travelling horizontally with the wind, would smash the propellers to pieces as effectively as shrapnel, kicked out his left foot, turned the control-column, and then dragged it back into his right thigh. The "Vandal" turned and sped away like a leaf before the storm.

The island disappeared from sight instantly, for they were now travelling downwind at a terrific rate. Presently they passed the schooner, scudding under bare poles through the raging spindrift. Another island flashed below in a whirl of white-lashed green and brown; a cloud of palm fronds, branches and debris swirled high into the air and trailed away like smoke over the open sea.

The pilot caught his breath. Ericson and his schooner were doomed, for an island with its jagged reef lay right across their path. It looked as if Bob's box would merely change its position on the bottom of the sea. He tried hard to visualise the map in an effort to remember what land, if any, lay ahead of them. Fortunately the "Vandal's" tanks were nearly full, and at their present speed they could cover a thousand miles, or more, if necessary.

The hours passed slowly. From time to time islands swept by below in a blur of writhing palms and foam-lashed rock, and the pilot scrutinized each one anxiously for a possible anchorage, knowing that they were now too far away from Gospel Island to return, even if the storm abated. Most of the islands held lagoons, some on the lee-ward side, but the floating and air-borne debris made landing out of the question. He was prepared to land anywhere that would afford a reasonably safe anchorage, where they could wait until the typhoon had passed or blown itself out, and then look for an inhabited island from which to learn their position. Already the storm was abating, or had shifted its course.

"What was in the box?" yelled Algy in the pilot's ear, but Biggles was not listening.

With outstretched finger he pointed ahead to where a long dark coastline stretched across their path. At one place it bayed into a wide estuary, with a river winding like a silver thread behind it into the grey distance. A long bungalow with several outbuildings stood on the edge of a sheltered backwater. As the pilot throttled back and dropped lower he could see a motor-boat with a Union Jack at the bow moored near by.

"Where are we?" he yelled, as he taxied up to the bank, where a man in white ducks, with several natives in uniform, stood awaiting them.

"Fly River, New Guinea. My name's Davidson. I'm the Resident Magistrate. Come in. You another one of these record-breakers?"

"We've just established a record from Gospel Island to here that will take some beating," observed the pilot soberly.

"Never mind records; what I want to know is, what was in the box?" broke in Algy, impatiently.

"Box? Oh, yes—a picture."

"A picture?" stammered Algy uncomprehendingly.

"Yes, a little oil-painting in a gold frame of a girl—Bob's wife, I expect. That was his treasure," added the pilot quietly, passing his hand wearily over his face.

CHAPTER 7

SAVAGES AND WINGS

THE TINY rose-pink early-morning clouds were fast fading in the turquoise sky as the tropical sun mounted rapidly above the horizon. Already its outflung rays were striking the palm-tops and the hills beyond in white bars of heat as Biggles and Algy left their hotel in Port Moresby, New Guinea, whither they had made their way after being driven far from their course by the typhoon.

Unhurriedly they strolled towards the beach to make the daily visit of inspection to the "Vandal" before proceeding to Government House to report their presence and pay their respects to the Governor of the Island.

In the lattice-like shade of a group of palms a man was lying, chin cupped in the palm of his hand, looking steadfastly at the "Vandal" as it rode the gentle swell near the shore. He was dressed in a loose cotton shirt, open at the throat, and drill trousers that had once been white but that were now creased and soiled by long service. Canvas shoes were thrust loosely on his feet.

It struck Algy that he must have been good-looking before dissipation and fever left their unmistakable marks upon his careworn face.

"This is the fellow who was hanging about the hotel lounge last night, isn't it?" he murmured in an undertone to Biggles as they drew level.

The pilot nodded. "Yes," he said quietly, "and do you know, I can't get away from the idea that I've seen him before somewhere, but I'm dashed if I can remember where."

They were about to pass when the man rose to his feet and came towards them. "That's your machine out there, isn't it?" he asked in a tired but cultured voice.

"It is," admitted Biggles. "Why?"

"Oh, nothing, really. I was interested, that's all; I haven't seen an aeroplane so close before. I used to be a bit of an engineer before I—well, you can see how things are now. I wonder if you would show me over it sometime?"

"Certainly, only too pleased," replied Biggles readily. "I'm going aboard presently; come and look round, by all means. In fact, Algy," he went on, turning to his partner, "if you don't mind going to see the old man alone I might as well look over her now, before the sun gets up. There are two or three little jobs I want to do and there is no need for us both to go up the hill."

"Righto," agreed Algy. "I'll come back and join you here; I shan't be more than half an hour. Cheerio."

A shock-headed Papuan, his skin gleaming under a new coat of oil and with a scarlet flower tucked behind his ear, paddled Biggles and his new acquaintance out to the machine.

The stranger looked about him with interest. "What are all these things?" he asked, pointing to the row of dials on the instrument board, and for nearly half an hour he listened in rapt attention while the pilot explained, with professional enthusiasm, the functions of the instruments and showed him how the starter and the wheels operated.

"Mind your head," said Biggles, as the stranger turned to look at the passenger accommodation.

Obediently the other ducked through the low doorway and then stood upright. Biggles bent low to follow. As he put his head down he remembered with a spasm of anger where he had seen the stranger before.

"Why——?" he began, and even as the world exploded inside his head in a sheet of purple flame that faded slowly to blackness he knew that the man had struck him. He pitched forward limply on his face and lay still.

Algy, wending his way slowly down the hillside from Government House, saw the "Vandal" swing slowly round until she faced the slight sea breeze, skim lightly over the blue water, and rise like a gull into the sun-soaked sky. "Must be giving him a joy-ride, the generous cuss," he soliloquised casually, but his brow puckered in surprise as the machine swung round towards the land and then struck off on a steady course towards the blue mountains in the distance. Puzzled, he watched it until it was a mere speck in the sky, and then, deep in thought, returned to the beach, where he flung himself down on the sand to await its return.

An hour passed slowly. Smyth, their mechanic, joined him, but could offer no solution to the mystery. Another two hours passed in doubt and vague speculation, and then Algy rose briskly to his feet.

"He's down," he said tersely. "He hadn't four hours' petrol on board; I'd better go and see the Governor."

II

Biggles's first conscious realisation as he slowly opened his eyes was that his head ached unmercifully; he next perceived that he was lying on the floor of the cabin, but it was not until he tried to raise his arm to his head to feel the extent of the damage that he made the painful and annoying discovery that his wrists and ankles were firmly tied. At the same moment the roar of the engine died away suddenly, and the floor tilted at an angle which told him they were gliding down. He tried to raise himself high enough to see out of the cabin-windows, but it was impossible, and his lips turned dry at the thought of a forced landing in his present position

He breathed a sigh of relief and then muttered an exclamation of surprise as the wheels touched solid ground and rumbled slowly to a standstill. The engine was switched off; the door of the cabin opened and the stranger stood before him.

"What's the idea, Dawne?" said Biggles coldly.

"You remember me, eh?" replied the other.

"I remembered you a trifle too late," admitted Biggles. "You were at Calshot, weren't you, on a Short Service Commission?"

"You ought to know," replied the other grimly.

"Why?"

"You were President of the Court that smashed me."

Biggles opened his eyes wide in astonishment.

"Yes, I remember," he said slowly. "You were court-martialled for cashing dud cheques. It was some time ago—I had forgotten it."

"I haven't," returned Dawne curtly. "Well, I don't bear you any malice for that; but listen. I need hardly tell you that I've a very good reason for coming here. A journey overland would have taken me three months and cost a lot more money than I'm ever likely to get. Moreover, I didn't want anybody else about, which is another reason why I couldn't bring a party. I couldn't come alone except this way because, as you no doubt know, the local gentry have a penchant for head-hunting, and hiking in these woods is neither a pleasant nor a profitable pastime. Naturally, I never thought I should have the opportunity of flying here. I nearly pitched you the whole yarn last night in the hope that you would carve in with me; in fact, I would have done if I could have believed that you would have fallen into line. But I knew you wouldn't."

"Still crooked, eh?" observed Biggles.

"Yes, and likely to be," admitted Dawne. "Don't get personal though; that won't help you. Keep quiet and I'll give you a break. When I've finished here I'll turn you loose. I shall fly back, but not to Moresby. With a bit of luck you might get back to Moresby in a month or two, and by that time I shall be well out of the way. I'll give you a gun if you'll give me your word that you won't use it against me until I get off the ground."

"Your generosity staggers me," sneered Biggles.

"I'll stagger you with something else if you try to be funny. I'm no murderer, Bigglesworth, but I'm not going to stand any nonsense; this is the first real chance I've had since I was smashed."

"How about cutting these straps," suggested Biggles, indicating his bound wrists.

"I will if you'll give me your parole," offered the other.

"I'm dashed if I do," replied Biggles through set teeth.

"As you like," nodded Dawne, with a shrug. "I'm moving off now; shall be back in a couple of hours or so. Cheerio!"

Biggles made no reply. For some time he lay still, trying to think out a plan of action, but there seemed little he could do. His wrists were tightly bound, and try as he would he found it impossible to loosen them; neither was there a single projection inside the hull against which he could chafe his bonds in the hope of fraying them. He had no idea of where they were or how far they were from Port Moresby nor could he ascertain whether they were on a beach or in a glade in the forest, although the shrill cries of parrots suggested the latter. The heat in the cabin was stifling and the hours passed slowly.

It was with some relief that he heard the returning footsteps of his abductor. The outside door of the cabin was opened and the ex-officer swung a heavy bag inside. Perspiration streamed down his face, which was flushed with heat and excitement.

"Do you know what that is?" he asked, with a grin.

"I neither know nor care," answered Biggles coldly.

"I'll show you." So saying, Dawne opened the top of the bag and inserted his hand; withdrawing it, he allowed a gleaming yellow stream to trickle through his fingers. "Gold-dust," he muttered in a voice hoarse with triumph.

In spite of his precarious position, Biggles stared incredulously.

" One more load like that and I'm through," went on Dawne. "Shan't be long."

The door closed again and Biggles heard the footsteps recede into the distance. For an hour all was quiet except for the occasional raucous cry of a bird or chatter of a monkey, and the pilot lay lost in thought, trying to solve the desperate problem with which he was faced. Subconsciously he heard a slight thud on the outside of the hull, as if a twig had dropped on it, but he paid little attention. The prospect of being left to struggle back to Port Moresby on foot appalled him. He knew little of the country, but sufficient to understand that not even an experienced prospector with a knowledge of the native dialects would lightly undertake such a task alone. The jungle, except for native tracks, was impenetrable, swarming with leeches, poisonous snakes, and centipedes. The natives, head-hunters and cannibals to a man were the most treacherous in the world. The rivers were the only highways, and except for the rare visit of an armed trader or government official were used only by the native canoes and crocodiles.

No, the prospect was not pleasant. Dawne's proposal to turn him loose was little better than a death-sentence, yet he could understand the ex-officer's disinclination to take him back to Port Moresby, where the arm of the law would speedily upset his plans. At intervals he heard the soft thud on the outside of the hull that he had heard before, and he wondered vaguely if an inquisitive monkey was exploring the machine. A sudden splintering blow brought him back to realities with a start, and he stared in petrified horror at something that had appeared in the cabin wall just above his face. It was the business end of a spear, nine inches of gleaming steel, still quivering. Another sharp thud on the other side of the cabin made him turn quickly to where an unmistakable arrowhead projected through the thin woodwork of the hull. He noted the dirty brown point and recalled the Papuan's notorious habit of poisoning his arrows. He shuddered, and then a gleam of hope flashed in his eyes. It was the work of a moment to raise his feet and cut the cord that bound them on the razor-edge of the spearhead. Scrambling to his knees, he severed the cords that tied his wrists and worked his numb fingers to restore the circulation.

He risked a cautious peep out of the cabin-window. The machine was standing under a large tree on a wide but undulating grassy plateau. Turning, he looked through the opposite window and saw that he was within fifty yards of the jungle. There were no signs of natives. Above him the parakeets swung lazily by bill and claw in the tree, over which a cascade of bougainvillæa spread like a purple stain. There were no more arrows; no scene could have appeared more peaceful, but he knew that from the sylvan wall of the forest many bestial eyes were fixed on the amphibian in hate and fear. Again the pilot turned towards the open ground on the other side to ascertain the best direction for a take-off, and he knew at once why the arrows had ceased. Dawne, with a bag slung over his shoulder, was hurrying across the plateau, perhaps a hundred yards distant.

Biggles moved swiftly. He dived through into the pilot's seat, whirled the self-starter, and then yelled as the engine came to life.

"Look out!" he shouted to the approaching man, who, when the engine started, stopped dead in his tracks, then dropped the bag and raced towards the machine. He swerved like a rugby-player as a flight of arrows whistled from the brushwood, and, crouching low, sprinted for the machine, now taxi-ing slowly towards him.

"Come on! You've made it," yelled Biggles.

Dawne, now thoroughly conscious of his danger, emptied his revolver into the undergrowth as he ran, and then dived under the wing of the machine to reach the door of the cabin. Even as he reached the door he stumbled and pitched forward on to his face, with the handle of a throwing-spear projecting from between his shoulder-blades.

Biggles turned stone-cold at the sight and acted purely on impulse. White-faced, he snatched the throttle back, dived under the low doorway, flung open the cabin door and dragged the fallen man inside. As he slammed the door behind him there was a yell from the wood and a shower of arrows struck the machine. There was another yell as the natives, seeing their prey about to escape, broke cover and charged.

Biggles darted back to the pilot's seat, and thrust the throttle wide open, just as the leading native reached the tail and aimed a blow at it with an axe, which, had it reached its mark, would have cut the empennage in halves; but he staggered back with an animal bark of alarm as the full slipstream of the propeller smote him.

The next few seconds, as the machine bumped with swiftly increasing speed over the rough ground, seemed an eternity of time to the pilot, and he relaxed limply with reaction as it lifted at last and soared skyward.

For a minute or two he held on his course, wondering which direction to take. Dawne was in the cabin, probably dying, but he could not leave the controls to help him or ask him where they were. On all sides stretched the forest, dark and forbidding. Almost immediately below, a fairly wide river lay like a carelessly dropped grey thread among the trees. In the distance to his left towered the jagged peaks of a mountain range, while far away to the right a broader river twisted and coiled upon itself a hundred times as it meandered towards the sea. But which was the nearest way to the sea? Biggles did not know, but with the ever-present possibility of a forced landing in his mind he headed instinctively towards the river, but before he reached it the smell of petrol made him look around in grey-faced anxiety. Petrol was on the floor, and the feathered end of an arrow projecting from the main tank told its own story.

The engine spluttered and faded out just as he reached the river, and he switched over to the gravity tank, which allowed him another twenty minutes' grace. It was impossible to tell which way the river flowed, but he turned the nose of the machine towards its broader end in the hope of reaching the sea, knowing that the nearer he was to the coast the safer he would be. He breathed a sigh of relief as presently the sea rose up on the horizon, but he was still some distance away when the steady roar of his engine became an intermittent splutter and then died away completely. The propeller gave a final kick and then stopped.

The pilot coolly studied the river to pick out the best spot within range for the inevitable landing. There were several straight reaches, and he automatically chose the longest, which fortunately happened to be the one nearest the sea. At a thousand feet he passed over a native village standing on stilt-like legs in the mud on the edge of the river, and he noted with satisfaction that it seemed deserted.

The tree-tops were motionless, so he concluded that there was little wind, if any, to be taken into account, and he flattened out confidently over the middle of the river. He skimmed over a great tree floating in the water and hoped desperately that there were no more; but his fears were groundless. The "Vandal" surged slowly to a standstill on the muddy water, and then commenced to float slowly downstream with the current. The pilot could do no more; he was even powerless to reach the bank, so after a swift glance around he hurried through into the cabin.

Dawne was lying on his side on the floor just as he

had left him. His face was ashen, but his eyes were open.

"Don't take it out," he said quietly, as he saw the pilot's eyes turn towards the spear in his back. "It will be all over if you do. It will soon be all over, anyway," he went on, "but before I go topsides I want to apologise to you, Biggleswórth——"

"Don't worry about that, Dawne," said Biggles softly, as he folded his jacket and placed it under the wounded man's head. "I'm sorry I couldn't make Moresby, but they holed my tank."

"Where are we now?" asked Dawne.

"On the river," replied Biggles.

"Do you mean the big river east of where I landed?"

Biggles nodded. A drum began beating fitfully in the bush not far away.

"You'll be all right then, if you are fairly near the sea," went on Dawne. "Most of the villages are friendly here."

There was silence for a few minutes, and the pilot, squatting on the floor, watched the stricken man compassionately.

"Just my luck," muttered the ex-pilot bitterly. "I *would* get this just as I had my hands on that." His eyes sought the bag of gold-dust lying on the floor. "I never did have much luck," he concluded ruefully.

"It's tough, very tough, I'll admit," agreed Biggles, "but you were asking for trouble the way you went to work."

"There wasn't any other way," muttered the wounded man.

"How did you know it was there?" asked Biggles curiously.

Dawne's face twisted into a ghost of a smile. "Listen," he said; "I'll tell you." A spasm of pain shook him and a bubble of blood seeped from a corner of his mouth.

"Don't talk if it hurts you," said Biggles quickly.

"I'll tell you—I'd rather someone like you had it—one of the old crowd—you know what I mean. It sort of finished me when I got chucked out," went on the dying man pathetically. "I didn't cash those cheques for myself. A girl—bah!—what does it matter?" He paused reflectively and then continued: "Kelly found the gold first, up there; he said the river-bed was full of it. He sold out to the British Alluvial Company and they sank a hundred thousand quid on a dredger. I got the job as under-manager, not because I knew the job, but because there was no other white man handy. Angus McReady was manager. He knew his job, but he was always too drunk to take much interest in it. The rest were boys—nearly all straight from the bush. At first the gold came up; then it stopped suddenly. I couldn't understand it, but there was no getting away from it; there wasn't enough to pay expenses. After a bit the company packed up, and that was that.

"A couple of years later, when I was down at Darwin, I ran into one of the boys who had worked for us; he had signed a labour contract with a sugar firm there. We talked about the mine and he told me how he used to scrub the plates down every morning and evening.

I couldn't make out what he meant at first, but after a bit I got the drift of what had happened."

The dying man paused, then went on.

"You know how the silt comes up and goes over the baffle plates to catch the gold dust? You don't? Well, it doesn't matter. The plates are treated with a solution of mercury to make the gold stick to them. Well, this poor ignorant fool didn't know what it was all about. He thought the machinery was a sort of god, and kept scrubbing the gold off the plates to keep them clean. Sort of thing a native would do. No wonder we weren't getting any metal! Every time he scrubbed the plates he washed a pile of gold down into the silt. Well, there it was, and I knew that if I could get back I should find big patches of dust in the silt, which would be easy enough to wash out. The dredger and plenty of tools had been left behind because they weren't worth the cost of labour to bring them, anyway.

"I worked a passage to Moresby and there I stuck. I daren't tell anybody about what I had discovered; I should have got nothing from the company, because they would have said I should have spotted what was going on at the time—and so I should, if it comes to that. No, my game was to get the gold myself, which would have been easy enough if I had had a bit of money for porters, but I hadn't. Then you rolled up, and that gave me an idea. I knew all about the plateau up there which I could land on. I had to take a chance that you didn't know me in order to find out about the controls, which were new to me, so I hung about the hotel—to give you a chance to speak if you recognised me. I soon saw that you didn't—you know the rest."

The stricken man was breathing with difficulty, and it was clear to Biggles that the end was not far off. "All right, old lad, take it easy; perish the gold, anyway," he said sympathetically, looking at the ghastly thing in Dawne's back.

"If you pull it out—I shall bleed to death—in a minute—I've seen it—before," gasped the dying man. "Shan't be long—anyway. Well—that's the tale," he went on. "I'd no money—no partner—no—nothing. But I—got it. It's later than I—thought—or else—getting dark early."

Biggles looked through the cabin window at the blazing afternoon sunshine, but said nothing. For a few minutes there was silence in the cabin. From outside came only the gasping grunt of a crocodile and the distant throbbing of a drum.

" 'S getting dark," said the dying man again. "Couldn't go alone—pity—had to go—through with it——" he moaned feebly, his mind wandering. "You still here—Bigglesworth—don't leave me—in the—dark."

"All right, laddie, I'm here," said Biggles thickly.

"Can't see you—not in the dark like this. Can't see . . . no flying tonight—better get flares out . . . climbing too fast . . . too dark . . . Pauline——"

The words faded into a mere whisper and the head dropped limply sideways.

Biggles rose to his feet, passed his hand wearily over his face, and stared unseeingly through the cabin window.

Presently he noticed that the machine was stationary, caught on the overhanging branches of a tree near the bank. He climbed out on to the hull, and was about to try to free it when a distant sound caught his ear. It was the unmistakable chug-chug-chug of a motor-boat. He listened intently for a moment; the boat was coming nearer.

Presently it chugged its way round the bend of the river, and he made out Algy, the District Magistrate, and two native police in the Government launch.

"Bit of luck for me your turning up like this," he observed as the motor-boat drew level.

"No luck about it," returned the D.M., smiling. "We've known where you were since you took off."

Biggles stared at him unbelievingly. "How?" he retorted incredulously.

"Hark!" said the D.M., raising his finger.

Biggles listened.

Tom-tom — tom-tom — tom-a-tom — tom-tom — came the sullen, barbaric voice of a drum in the bush not far away; and then, like an echo in the far distance, *tom-a-tom — tom-tom — tom-a-tom — tom-tom —* came another, and yet another.

"Bush telegraph," said the D.M. laconically. "Every native within fifty miles knows by now that we've found you. Dawne's dead, I expect? H'm. Thought so. We weren't sure which of you it was, when we got the message over the drums."

"Which reminds me I've a message to send myself," observed Biggles casually. "Let's get back."

"Message? Who to?" asked Algy in surprise.

"To my bank," replied Biggles sagely. "I happened to notice in an old paper I was reading a day or two ago that British Alluvial one-pound shares were quoted at one shilling. They'll jump to fifty when the company knows what I know."

"Be a good thing to buy a few," suggested Algy.

"That's just what I thought," grinned Biggles.

CHAPTER 8

THE ORIENTAL TOUCH

FROM THE comfortable cockpit of the "Vandal" Biggles looked down dispassionately upon the sun-soaked waters of the Indian Ocean two thousand feet below as he sped northwards on the eight-hundred-mile trip from Penang to Rangoon.

A fortnight had elapsed since their departure from New Guinea. They had made their way by easy stages to Lombok and Surabaya, made famous as the landing-grounds of record-breaking pilots on the Australia run, and thence to Jakarta, the terminus of the K.L.M. grand trunk airline to the Dutch East Indies. From there they had flown to Singapore, where they had been guests of the Royal Air Force Flying-boat Squadron stationed there while the "Vandal" was given a quick overhaul by Service mechanics, and then on to Penang. After a brief stay they had left that morning for Rangoon, the next port of call on their homeward journey.

In the distance, on their right, lay the palm-fringed, surf-washed beach of the Malay Peninsula, with the dark-green forest stretching away behind it. To their left was the ocean, an infinite expanse of blue reaching to the far horizon; not a ripple broke its surface to give a hint of the seething fury soon to come in the wake of the inevitable monsoon. A short distance ahead were the outlying sentinels of the Mergui Archipelago, the long line of islands that lie like a chain of emeralds set in turquoise for more than four hundred miles along the western seaboard of Malaya.

For an hour they held steadily on their course, fresh islands rising up over the horizon to meet them as others slipped away astern. At one of them, rather larger than the rest, a junk rode at anchor in a small almost landlocked lagoon. From sea-level it must have been out of sight of passing ships, but from the air its limp sulphur-yellow sail gleamed like a ray of gold amid the encircling blue.

For a few minutes, while they were passing over the island, the pilot watched it curiously; he could see the crew standing on the beach watching him, and half envied them their simple existence far from the turmoil of civilisation. Presently the island slid away behind as the "Vandal" roared on through the crystal-clear atmosphere, and with its passing the junk became a half-forgotten memory.

It was perhaps a quarter of an hour later that Algy, starting up out of a day-dream, noticed the pilot staring hard at something that lay ahead and below. Following his gaze, he had no difficulty in picking out the object of his partner's attention on the limpid water. At first he watched it disinterestedly, but as he held his gaze a puzzled expression crept over his face, and shading his eyes from the glare of the sun he subjected the object to a long and searching scrutiny. He looked up and his eyes met those of the pilot. He raised his eyebrows inquiringly and turned his thumb down with a grimace. Instantly the roar of the engine faded away and the amphibian tilted down in a long glide towards a white object that floated on the surface of the water. It seemed to be motionless now, although Algy was quite certain that he had seen it move just before the pilot throttled back; in fact, it almost seemed as if it had raised itself up in the water and waved to them.

Slowly the machine dropped lower and still the thing did not move, but at two hundred feet there was no longer any doubt. It was what both pilots had suspected, but could hardly believe: the body of a man floating in the water. Biggles flew past once very low, to make quite certain, and then, swinging round in a steep bank, flattened out and dropped lightly on the water, coming to rest not more than a hundred feet from their objective.

Algy hurried through the cabin and threw the door open as they taxied alongside.

"Take it easy," cautioned Biggles, as they reached out for the flimsy raft on which the man was lying. "He may sink if we capsize him. Great Scott! Poor fellow! What a mess he's in," he muttered compassionately as he noted the sun-blistered skin of the naked man. "Gently does it—good—get the brandy out of my case, Smyth; look sharp; he's all in."

Carefully they laid the unconscious man on the floor of the cabin.

Algy gasped suddenly. "He's a Chink!"

Biggles paused in the act of unscrewing an oil-can to

stare for a moment in surprise. "You're right; so he is," he agreed. "Well, we can't help that—we might have expected it; I'll pour some of this oil on his shoulders if you'll get the brandy between his teeth—steady; don't overdo it or you'll drown him—that's enough; he's coming round. You'll do—get him a beaker of water."

The unconscious man stirred and looked up with lack-lustre eyes at the three faces bending over him.

"Take a pull of this," invited Biggles, offering the water-bottle and raising his head.

The Chinaman seized the water-bottle eagerly and poured the contents down his parched throat.

"That'll do for the present," went on the pilot, taking the bottle from his hands.

"Thanks," gasped the rescued man.

Biggles raised his eyebrows. "Speekee Engleesh, eh?" he inquired.

"Not that sort," replied the exhausted man in a cultured voice, with a ghost of a smile.

Algy glanced at his partner in amused surprise, but the Chinaman intercepted the look. "I was at Oxford," he explained.

"The dickens you were!" ejaculated Biggles. "Well, take it quietly for a minute and then we'll talk."

Presently the rescued man was sitting propped up against the hull, wrapped in Algy's dressing-gown. "What ship is this?" he asked curiously, glancing around.

"It isn't a ship; it's an aeroplane," replied Biggles.

"Ah, of course. I had just given up hope and was about to let go of my raft when I saw you coming. I suppose I must have fainted then. Where are you going?"

"Rangoon!"

"Must I go to Rangoon?"

"I'm afraid so."

The Chinaman meditated awhile, and then: "Are you on a record-breaking voyage?" he asked.

"No," replied Biggles, smiling. "We are just beetling along towards home, that's all."

"I see." Again the Chinaman pondered. "I wonder"—he went on hesitatingly—"whether it would be too much to ask you to put me ashore as quickly as possible. If you would consider taking me to Penang, so much the better. Do you think me impertinent, but I should be quite prepared to recompense you for any inconvenience or change of plan it may involve."

Biggles shook his head. "We can't do that," he said. "It's a long way back and would cost a lot of money for fuel alone."

"I have a lot of money," observed the rescued man quietly. "If it is only a matter of expense——"

"How did you get in this mess?" interrupted Biggles.

"Li Chi," replied the Chinaman briefly, as if that were sufficient explanation.

"What's that got to do with it?" exclaimed Biggles in surprise. "I thought Li Chi was a kind of fruit; I had some in Singapore."

"It is," agreed the other, "but you are evidently a stranger to these parts or you would know it is also the soubriquet of the worst character that ever sailed these seas, a pirate, a smuggler, and a thief. He sank my ship and then threw me into the sea, to the sharks—as he thought."

"Evidently a gentleman to be avoided," observed Biggles. "He doesn't run a junk with a yellow sail, by any chance, does he?"

The Chinaman started. "Have you seen such a ship?" he asked eagerly.

"Yes; we passed it about a quarter of an hour ago, in the lagoon of the long island about twenty-five miles to the south."

"Raffa Island: it is he," grated the Chinaman between his teeth, clenching and unclenching his hands. "Let me tell you," he went on quickly. "My name is Hoi Sing, and my father is a rich man, a merchant in Shanghai. I was on my way to India with a valuable cargo in one of our ships when I met this fiend. He attacked my ship and sank it while we were fetching fresh water from an island. Most of my men were ashore, but I was captured, taken out to sea and then thrown overboard. He should have killed me first," he concluded, with a curious smile.

"What do you propose to do?" asked Biggles sympathetically.

"If you take me to Rangoon I can do nothing," went on the other quickly, "for he will hide among the hundreds of islands between here and the Philippines, as he always does, and where he cannot be found. If you would allow me to hire your aeroplane for a day, or perhaps two days, I can outwit him. I don't mind what it costs as long as I can lay hands upon this villain—three thousand—five thousand dollars—I don't mind."

Biggles made a quick mental calculation. "That's all right with me," he agreed, "but you won't mind my mentioning that you don't look particularly affluent at the moment."

The Chinaman flushed slightly. "I quite understand that," he said at once. "I know I must look like a beggar, but it is not so. First of all I must have money and clothes. Take me, then, to Penang, where my uncle will furnish me with all I need and I will pay you in advance. Then all I ask you to do is to transport me and my men to the farther end of the island where Li Chi's junk is at anchor. You may leave the rest to me. In my country we have our own way of dealing with brigands."

"So I understand," said Biggles dryly. "How many men have you?"

"About fourteen or fifteen, I think."

"We could take them in three loads, Algy," said Biggles, turning to his partner. "It shouldn't take long; it isn't far between the islands. We can each take a rest while the other takes a load across."

Five minutes later they were in the air, retracing their course to Penang.

II

"I shall have to ask you to take a message to my uncle," said their passenger, half apologetically, as they taxied in on arrival. "I cannot very well go ashore like this."

"No, you can't," agreed Biggles. "Scribble a note and I'll take it along. Algy, you see about getting the tanks filled up while I'm away; better get a few spare tins inside as well, if you can. I shan't be long."

He was back within an hour, bringing with him not only a chest of clothes and two heavy canvas bags that jingled promisingly, but Hoi Sing's uncle, who had insisted on seeing his unfortunate nephew.

In swift Chinese Hoi Sing explained what had transpired, and then counted out the sum agreed upon for the hire of the machine.

"Well, let's get away," said Biggles at last; "we've a lot to do yet."

The old Chinaman hurried ashore, and once more they headed towards the scene of Hoi Sing's disaster. They passed the yellow-sailed junk on the way, and the Chinaman eyed it with cold hostility. He directed them to a smaller island on the horizon and then requested them to land in a sheltered bay, which he assured them offered a safe anchorage. There was no sign of Hoi Sing's crew as they taxied in, but in response to a peculiar whistle from the Chinaman, who, now clad in a blue silk kimono, stood up conspicuously in the rear cockpit, a shrill babble of voices came from the jungle.

A number of men broke cover, pointed, called to others, and then ran down to the beach in obvious delight. Biggles eyed them with disapproval, for a more unsavoury crowd he had never seen. Of the fourteen who waded out to meet them nearly all were Chinese, but there were one or two Malay dyaks, armed with the inevitable kris, and a negro. For a few minutes he watched the scene, unable to understand a word of the conversation, but able to follow

Hoi Sing's dramatic explanation of his reappearance by his gestures. He noted the open-eyed amazement of the crew as Hoi Sing described how he had been picked up out of the sea; the doubtful hesitation as he told them they were to be taken to another island in the aeroplane, and the sharp intakes of breath when he explained the reason.

Biggles called the Chinaman's attention to the sun, already past its zenith, and the first half-dozen passengers were quickly in their place. Relinquishing his seat to Algy, he went ashore with Smyth to await the return of the "Vandal." Three journeys were necessary, but by evening Hoi Sing and his crew had been safely transported across the intervening stretch of water, and Biggles was wishing his first and only Oriental client goodbye.

"I can never thank you enough for what you have done for me today," said Hoi Sing courteously. "May I ask you and your friend to accept this?"—he handed the pilot a tiny package, sealed with wax. "You may never know how much I am in your debt," he went on, "but I must ask you, however, not to unwrap my present until you reach Rangoon. Goodbye."

Biggles thrust the packet into his pocket and watched the retreating figure of the Chinaman in quiet amusement. "Queer cove," he observed. "Well," he went on with a change of tone, "let's get the machine up on the beach for the night; we'll push on to Rangoon tomorrow."

Just before dawn Bigglesworth was awakened by the distant rattle of musketry.

"What's all that din?" muttered Algy drowsily in the darkness.

"It sounds as if Li Chi's getting his beauty-sleep disturbed," said Biggles sleepily.

"Serves him right," grunted Algy philosophically, relapsing again into slumber.

Two days later Biggles sat on the palm-shaded verandah of the Hotel Mandalay in Rangoon, plotting the course of the next "leg" of their journey, which would take them to Calcutta. Beside him Algy was reclining comfortably in a long cane chair, reading a local newspaper he had picked up in the lounge. Biggles, happening to glance up, noticed that his face wore a curious expression and he instinctively leaned over to see what was intriguing him.

He stiffened in his chair as his eyes fell on a paragraph-heading in bold type on the front page. There were only two words—Li Chi—and he read on with interest.

"News of what must be one of the most astounding sea mysteries of recent years has been revealed by a wireless message just received from Singapore.

"As published in this journal a few days ago, the authorities were recently informed of the position of the notorious pirate Li Chi, who was known to be en route for India with a quantity of opium. This information was furnished by Captain Hoi Sing, whose junk, with its conspicuous yellow sail, is a frequent visitor to this port.

"It will be remembered that Captain Hoi Sing was once an associate of Li Chi, but left him on a difference of opinion and subsequently received an amnesty from the Government in return for certain services.

"As a result of the information, Captain Starkey, of the Government sloop *Cormorant*, was able to intercept Li Chi, and after a swift engagement succeeded in capturing the junk and its captain. Captain Starkey reported that a number of the crew had put off in a small boat at the last moment and succeeded in reaching an island, where, as they had taken refuge in the thick jungle, it was not thought worth while to pursue them. Captain Starkey confiscated the contraband and took the junk in tow, but it shortly afterwards sank in deep water from the damage it had received.

"That same night, while being escorted to Captain Starkey's cabin for interrogation, Li Chi sprang overboard, presumably preferring to die rather than suffer inevitable imprisonment. The sloop was at once stopped and a search made, but as the pirate could not be found it was thought that he had been drowned or become the prey of the sharks that infest these waters.

"Yesterday, Captain Dupree, of the s.s. *Pacific*, put in at Raffa Island for fresh water. He reports by wireless to Singapore that Captain Hoi Sing and his entire crew have been murdered and lie dead on the beach. A later message states that the murdered Captain's junk, easily recognized by its yellow sail, has been seen sailing north-west before a fair wind, as if bound for an Indian port.

"It would seem that in some unaccountable manner Li Chi's crew succeeded in crossing from the island to which they escaped, to Raffa Island, a distance of about twenty-five miles, where they succeeded in overpowering Captain Hoi Sing and seizing his ship. The authorities are unwilling to accept this theory, pointing out that if it is correct the boats by which Li Chi's crew reached Raffa Island would still be there, whereas Captain Dupree states definitely that there is not a single boat on the island. Further, they are unable to reconcile the subsequent movements of the junk in proceeding towards India as if the pirates were still in possession of their illicit cargo, which, as previously stated, had been confiscated by Captain Starkey. It is, of course, impossible that a fresh supply of the forbidden opiate could have been obtained in the time at their disposal. We await subsequent developments with interest."

Biggles looked up and drew a deep breath, as his eyes met those of his partner. "That reminds me," he said in a strained voice, moistening his lips. He groped in his pocket and took out a tiny package sealed with wax. He tore it open impatiently. Two magnificent pink pearls rolled into the palm of his hand from a slip of paper. On the paper, in a small neat hand, was written:

A small token of my eternal gratitude,
LI CHI.

"What do you think was in that chest we fetched from Penang?" asked Biggles, speaking with difficulty.

"I'll give you two guesses," grinned Algy.

"I know the sooner we're out of this locality the happier I shall be," observed Biggles grimly.

CHAPTER 9

DOWN IN THE FOREST

BIGGLES glanced upwards approvingly at a sky of unbroken blue, as he taxied the "Vandal" into position for a take-off outside Rangoon harbour for the next "hop" of the journey which would, he hoped, bring them to Calcutta, with Akyab as an intermediate emergency landing-ground.

"I think we may risk the short cut," he told Algy, confidently, referring to a previous discussion as to whether or not they should follow the coast-line or cut across that part of Burma where the wandering Irrawaddy at last breaks up into a hundred mouths and leech-infested swamps, and where at least one British long-distance airman has met his death—a grim fact they had not overlooked.

"We'll take a chance," replied Algy philosophically, "but I don't mind admitting I shan't be happy until we hit the coast again; a forced landing in that country and we're sunk; that's where poor Hook——"

"All right—I know all about that," replied Biggles shortly. "If the weather was anything but perfect I wouldn't take the chance," he added, opening the throttle.

The rhythmic purr of the engine became a challenging roar and the machine sped across the sparkling blue waters of the Gulf of Martaban in a cloud of spray; then, as the pilot eased the control-column back, the churning wake fell away astern and the "Vandal" soared gracefully into the tropic sky, swinging round under a touch of the rudder-bar until the compass needle pointed east-north-east.

Biggles studied the ground ahead, where a dozen meandering streams lay like a carelessly dropped skein of silver ribbons across the inevitable paddy-fields. But the cultivation soon gave way to wilder country, and presently the "Vandal" was winging its way over dark-green virgin jungle and wide areas of bamboo and mangrove swamp.

For some time neither of the men in the cockpit spoke, but settled down to that curious condition which can only be described as semi-comatose-yet-wide-awake—the feeling of alert restfulness well known to all long-distance pilots.

Biggles, who had been staring thoughtfully ahead, suddenly fixed his gaze. A frown puckered his forehead. Algy, following his gaze, pulled the corners of his mouth down in an expression of annoyance.

The object of their attention would not have been immediately apparent to a passenger; indeed, nobody except perhaps a seaman or an airman would have noticed it. The peaks of the Arakan Yoma range that lay in their line of flight were now not quite so clear-cut as they had been a few moments before; that was all. Five minutes later, although they were appreciably nearer, the mountains had disappeared completely.

The pilot opened the throttle wide and began climbing for height in order to get above the mist into which they appeared to be heading, fervently hoping it would not develop into one of those opaque fogs which make flying in Farther India so treacherous. He looked back, but there was no escape that way; if anything, the conditions there were worse. He shrugged his shoulders resignedly as the landscape was slowly blotted out by billowing clouds of vapour. He was not particularly worried, for they were at least halfway to the coast on the other side of the peninsula, where over the warm water of the Indian Ocean the fog would certainly terminate as abruptly as if it had been chopped off with a knife. They were well above the mist and experienced no difficulty in maintaining their original course, and except for the unlikely event of engine failure they had nothing to fear.

Five minutes later, without a single warning splutter, the engines cut out dead.

Not by the slightest movement did the pilot at the control-column indicate that the cessation of noise, in the present atmospheric conditions, was as likely to prove as fatal as a death-sentence. The nose of the machine dropped as he eased the column forward in a glide towards the invisible earth below. And then, as quickly as they had stopped, the engines sprang to life again.

Biggles looked at his partner and his lips formed the words: "Petrol outlet."

Algy nodded, knowing perfectly well that with a clogged

petrol outlet from the tank their safe arrival was now in the hands of the gods. It might last until they reached the coast or it might not; foreign matter around the petrol outlet pipe can play strange tricks. They were not left long in suspense. Twice the engines cut out and each time they picked up again. Another brief interval and they went for the third and last time; the propellers stopped turning. The pilot dived as steeply as he dared with the throttle levers still forward in a forlorn hope that they might pick up again, but in vain, and the next moment they were enveloped in the enshrouding mist.

Biggles drew the control-column back until they were gliding almost at stalling point, and with his eyes on the altimeter waited for the inevitable crash; 7,000—6,000—4,000—2,000—the needle crept back inexorably on the dial, and still the cold grey mist enveloped them. The silence was uncanny.

"Tell Smyth not to jump," said the pilot coolly, and Algy, with set face, turned his head and passed back the instructions to their mechanic, who, with a wisdom born of experience, had already drawn his knees up to his chin and folded his arms over his face in anticipation of the coming shock. At five hundred feet by the instrument a dark shadow loomed below through the mist; a second later it became possible to see the ground.

"Forest," said Biggles shortly.

"Yes. No—water!" cried Algy, half rising in his seat.

The pilot made a swift turn that nearly flung Algy overboard, determined at all costs not to lose sight of that narrow lake that meant salvation.

For the next few seconds he circled in a tight S turn, side-slipped gently, and then dropped quietly on the unruffled surface of a sheet of water, the machine finishing its run within ten yards of a dark belt of mangroves.

For a little while nobody spoke; then Biggles passed his hand wearily over his face. "Seems to be our lucky day," he observed quietly.

Algy nodded. "You're right," he admitted limply. "I don't want another fright like that for a bit. It would be interesting to know just where we are," he added as an afterthought.

"It would," replied Biggles, "but I fancy we are better off here than we were upstairs. We can at least sit still until the fog lifts; there is plenty of room to get off again when it does. Hullo! We're drifting. Try to catch hold of something to hang on to while I help Smyth clear the outlet pipe."

A few minutes later he paused in his work to look at the place into which they had drifted—a long dark backwater with mangroves and occasional patches of the water-loving mipas-palms on either side, nearly meeting overhead. There was no question of going ashore even if they could have reached the bank, for the ground on each side was inundated as far as they could see and strewn with rotting skeletons of trees. Vivid-green moss clung to the roots and masses of grey lichen hung from the branches.

"Don't fall in," he warned Algy, who was trying to reach an overhanging bough; "there are certain to be crocs about—and things like that," he added, pointing to a large water-snake that glided along the trunk of a half-submerged tree at their approach.

"We're still drifting," observed Algy.

"It doesn't matter if we are," replied Biggles; "we shouldn't go far at this rate, anyway, and we can taxi back as soon as the pipe is cleared."

II

It was late in the afternoon, however, before the outlet had been unclogged, and the engines were once more giving their full revolutions. The mist had rolled away as suddenly as it had appeared, and without the slightest anxiety they commenced to taxi back up the dim avenue down which they had been slowly drifting for several hours.

"Stop her!" It was Algy who spoke, standing up in his seat and looking at the bank with a curious expression on his face. "We're wrong," he went on in a puzzled tone of voice; "we didn't come down here."

"Are you sure?" replied Biggles, with an uncomfortable twinge of alarm.

"Certain. We haven't passed that dead tree before—that one with the orchid growing on it. We should have taken the narrow turning at that last fork. Let's go back."

The machine was turned and they taxied slowly back over their course. They reached the fork to which Algy had referred, but a few minutes later were confronted by a triple fork, and, to add to their confusion, there were several turnings or tributaries on each side.

"I don't like this," muttered Biggles uneasily; "we

should have watched where we were going, but I think this is the one."

They set off up a new waterway, taxi-ing more quickly in their anxiety, but it narrowed until the wings of the machine were nearly touching the sombre trees on either side and they knew they were again mistaken. Without speaking, they turned the amphibian, not without difficulty, and were almost immediately confronted by a bewildering maze of forks and side-turnings. A fallen tree, half submerged, effectually barred any further progress in the path they had taken.

"We're lost," observed Biggles coolly, switching off the engine, "lost to the world. And we're here for the night, by the look of it," he added, nodding towards the sun, which, sinking in the west in a blaze of crimson glory, cast a ruddy glow over the black waters of the swamp.

"We had better see about making camp," suggested Algy, reaching out for an overhanging branch and pulling the machine towards the bank, which at this place seemed to offer a fairly secure foothold. "We may find the lagoon by cutting through here," he suggested.

"And lose our way back to the machine! Not if I know it," declared Biggles grimly. "Let's get a fire going to keep off the mosquitoes; take a can of petrol ashore and the suitcases to sit on."

III

Darkness fell with tropical suddenness and found them squatting round a fire in a little open space some fifteen or twenty yards from the amphibian. The ground was soft and quaked under their feet as they walked, but it was the best place they could find. It was devoid of any sort of grass or undergrowth, and the gnarled trunks of the encircling mangroves, distorted by the flickering firelight, assumed curious life-like forms and cast long serpentine shadows across the clearing.

Weird noises, in which the choking grunt of an alligator could alone be distinguished, came from the inky darkness outside the radius of firelight; something heavy was dragging itself through the ooze by the water's edge.

"This place gives me the creeps," muttered Algy in a low voice. "Let's get some more wood and build the fire up." He arose and reached up for a dead, overhanging bough. It broke off with a snap and shed an army of small living creatures over the ground around them, creatures that scuttled away with a faint rustling noise among the dead leaves. Biggles and Smyth sprang to their feet.

"Look what you're doing, you fool," snapped Biggles in a tense voice, reaching out for the fallen limb to drag it to the fire; but he sprang aside with a shuddering "Ugh!" "Look at that thing!" he gasped, pointing to a bloated foot-long centipede that had disengaged itself from the bark and was slithering away with a loathsome concertina-like movement. He laughed, a short uneasy laugh. "Let's take things quietly," he said, seating himself again by the fire.

They smoked for some time in silence. A great bat, silent as a shadow, wheeled once round the clearing and disappeared into the darkness whence it came.

"What's that?" ejaculated Algy suddenly.

Biggles followed the outstretched finger to where two red orbs glowed dully just outside the circle of light.

"Croc., I suppose," replied Biggles tersely.

Presently the eyes were joined by another pair, another, and yet another. Here and there smaller pairs of green lamps appeared, motionless, facing the fire. Before long they were in the centre of a circle of silent watchers.

Algy jumped to his feet, snatched a smouldering brand from the fire and hurled it with a shrill yell at a segment of the circle. Every light went out instantly as if they had been extinguished by a master-switch. Algy laughed, a high falsetto laugh. "Wretched things," he muttered as he sat down.

The lights switched on again at once: large eyes, small eyes, yellow, red, and green eyes, silent and unwinking.

Biggles rose abruptly. "I'm going to fetch the gun," he said shortly; "we'll see what a shot or two'll do."

"I'll come with you," said Algy quickly.

Smyth also rose to his feet, and without another word they followed the pilot to where the amphibian was moored. Something heavy slithered away in the darkness and an army of crabs on tall, stilt-like legs scuttled before them into the water as they reached the bank.

Biggles had raised his foot to step on board, but he flung himself backward with a sharp cry of alarm.

"What's that?" he muttered in a voice which he strove to keep steady.

Algy peered forward. Dimly in the gloom he could see a large black object piled up just behind the pilot's seat.

It was moving, very, very slowly, with a sinuous gliding movement.

Algy backed away quickly, clutching Biggles's arm. "Snake!" he said in a hoarse whisper. "What a size!"

For a moment they stood, staring, hesitating. "Let's get back to the fire," snapped Biggles.

"The blessed thing will soon be out if we don't do something about it," observed Algy. "Let's see if these leaves will burn—ah!" He nearly screamed as a great moth nearly struck him in the face as it whirled an erratic course across the clearing. "Curse this place!" he cried irritably, and began scraping a pile of fallen leaves together with his foot. He paused, bending low. "Biggles," he said in a strained voice, "what on earth are these things?"

The pilot struck a match and held it near the ground. "Leeches," he said thickly, "millions of 'em. Great Scott! We'll have to get out of here somehow."

"How—how?" cried Algy frantically.

"I don't know," admitted Biggles; "we must be hundreds of miles from the nearest—hark!"

The three airmen stood rigid, like figures carved in stone, frozen into attitudes of tense expectancy. Biggles flung up his arm as if to ward off a blow. "I'm mad," he muttered under his breath, "mad!"

Clear-cut in the silence of the tropic night came the bell-like notes of a piano, the vibrating waves of sound rising and falling in the majestic cadence of Elgar's "Salut d'Amour."

A long peal of hysterical laughter broke from Algy's lips.

The music stopped abruptly, in the middle of a bar.

"Stop that," snarled Biggles, swinging round at Smyth, who was muttering incoherently. Stooping swiftly he flung open his suitcase and took out a shirt. He broke a stick from a tree, bound the shirt round one end of it and then saturated it with petrol from the tin they had brought ashore. He thrust the improvised torch into the fire and then raised it like a blazing beacon high above his head. "Come on!" he cried, starting forward, and then stared unbelievingly at a man in immaculate evening dress who had stepped into the circle of light.

"What on earth are you fellows doing here?" asked a quiet, well-bred voice.

For a moment the airmen could only stand and stare. "Well—er—I'm not quite sure," blurted out Biggles. "We were flying—had a forced landing. We came down on a lake, or river, but drifted out of it and lost ourselves."

"The lake is just here, through the trees—so is my bungalow. The plantation is a bit lower down. I've just been down there, so I suppose that is why I didn't hear you land. My boy said something about an aeroplane in the fog, but I didn't believe him. By the way, where's your machine?"

"Just over here," replied Biggles, in a dazed voice, "but there's a very nasty passenger on board at the moment."

"What do you mean?"

"A snake of enormous dimensions has taken up its quarters behind the pilot's seat."

"A snake? Let's go and look," said the stranger, taking the torch from Biggles's hand.

The airmen followed him to the machine. He held the torch aloft and a chuckle came from his throat.

"Why, it's Penelope!" he said, stepping forward and fondling the snake's flat head affectionately. "What are you doing here, old girl? She's my pet python," he explained, "gentle as a kitten. She roosts in the bungalow; I have just let her out for her evening ramble. Come on; let's go and get a drink—come on, Penelope."

CHAPTER 10

THREE WEEKS

THE SUN was setting in a blaze of scarlet and gold over the Indian Ocean as Biggles slowly made his way through the heterogeneous throng of humanity in the Delhi Road, Karachi, towards the Orient Hotel, where he had left Algy, who, reposing near a punkah with an iced drink at his elbow, had declined Biggles's invitation to take a look round the town. Undeterred, Biggles had wended his way alone from street to street and was now returning to the Orient for dinner.

At the corner of Temple Square, with his eyes on a street carpetseller, rather than on his line of march, he collided violently with a slim, white-clad European who was coming in the opposite direction. The apology that rose automatically to his lips remained unuttered as he found himself staring into a rather tired face, upon which flashed a smile of instant recognition.

"Well, by the sacred turnbuckle of Saint Patrick, if it isn't Pat O'Neilson! Hallo, Pat!"

"Hullo, Biggles! what brings you to this part of the world; I heard you'd left the Service?"

Biggles nodded. "I have," he said. "I no longer aviate aircraft decorated with the red-white-and-blue target.

At the moment I'm beetling towards England, home and beauty in a rather dilapidated amphibian."

"Good heavens! Then it *was* you mixed up in that affair with Li Chi at Rangoon; there's been a queer tale going round about an aircraft helping him out, and I heard the name Bigglesworth mentioned as the pilot."

"I don't know how it's leaked out, but it's true enough," admitted Biggles. "It was I, and young Algy Lacey—you remember Algy? He's with me now. What are you doing here? You're not looking too good if I may say so."

A shadow flickered across the tired blue eyes of the Irishman, eyes that had once probed the skies of France from the cockpit of an R.A.F. Spitfire. "What about a spot of hospitality?" he suggested.

Biggles smiled. "Lead on Macduff. What's the trouble, Pat?" he continued when they had settled themselves in a quiet corner. "You look harassed."

The other shrugged his shoulders. "I am," he admitted. "We all are."

"Who's we?"

O'Neilson dropped his voice to a whisper. "Intelligence."

Biggles pursed his lips and raised his eyebrows. "So that's it," he muttered. "I might have guessed. Weren't you posted to H.Q. Intelligence in France after you were busted up by that Messerschmitt near Estree?"

O'Neilson nodded. "Sure," he said softly; "that was the way of ut, and here I am, still at ut."

"Ticklish job out here nowadays, I should think."

"It is, since the British bulldog lost his teeth or forgot

how to bite," muttered O'Neilson bitterly. "But it's the Great White Bear that worries us."

"Russia?"

O'Neilson flashed a swift, uneasy glance around that remained fixed on a short, swarthy, heavily moustached man who was just entering the saloon. Almost imperceptibly the Irishman turned his chair until his back was towards the newcomer. "Speak of the devil!" he breathed.

"Who's the enemy?" asked Biggles softly.

"He's the fly in the ointment, the thorn in the flesh; in other words, the Big Noise behind the Hammer and Sickle in this part of the world. We call him Ivan Nikitoff, because we think that's his real name, but he has many others."

"But I thought you people were experts at removing splinters," protested Biggles.

O'Neilson grimaced. "Used to be. It isn't so easy now, with a crowd in the operating theatre, so to speak, watching every move. That man is Russia's prize piece of furniture in the East. He holds the strings between Baghdad and Bombay, and when he pulls 'em things buzz. We've got a big show on at the moment over this Persian business, and he's the man who's going to spike our guns—if he can. Normally his headquarters are in Teheran, and his presence here means that he's on the job. And if you want to know the real cause of the furrow on my brow, well, he's it."

"Is that so?" mused Biggles reflectively. "Why not remove him to a safe place until it's all over?"

"How?"

"Don't ask me—that's your job. I should take him for a ride, like they do in America."

O'Neilson smiled wanly. "As crude as ever, I see. Can you see him stepping into an R.A.F. machine, or accepting our invitation to take a sea-cruise in one of our battleships?" he said. "Still, it would be worth something to have him out of the way."

"How much, I wonder?" said Biggles softly.

O'Neilson started, caught Biggles's eye, and then looked away quickly. Then he looked at his watch, thoughtfully. "What about having a bite with me at my club?" he suggested. "Algy won't miss you."

"Good idea," agreed Biggles.

II

The following morning Biggles was rudely awakened by the abrupt entry of Algy into his room, still in pyjamas, a cup of tea in one hand, and a newspaper in the other.

"What's all this nonsense?" demanded Algy, holding out the newspaper with an irritable flourish.

"What are you talking about?" inquired Biggles tersely.

"Who's responsible for this tripe?"

Biggles took the proffered paper, eyes on the paragraph indicated by his irate partner, and read:

WORLD-FLYERS IN KARACHI

Major James Biggleswortb, D.S.O., who had a brilliant record as a pilot during the war, landed yesterday at Karachi. His flight, which has already embraced more than half the globe, will be continued tomorrow towards England by a new route Istarain, Teheran, and the Black Sea ports. He is flying a Vickers "Vandal" amphibian aircraft with an assistant pilot and a mechanic. The airmen are staying at the Orient Hotel.

"Well," observed Biggles with a smile, as he looked up from the printed page, "what do you know about that?"

"Did you go crazy or something last night?"

Biggles looked pained. "Me crazy!" he protested. "Don't be foolish. Someone's seen our machine on the tarmac and done a bit of guessing; that's all there is to it."

"Well, let's push on, for heaven's sake, before all the fabric is stripped off the machine by souvenir-hunters. We'll be dogged to death by baboo photographers if we stay here, and if my guv'nor sees my mug in the papers he'll throw a fit; he hates publicity."

"So do I. All right; I'm ready when you are. Let's hit the breeze for Gwadir—I suppose we shall follow the Imperial route?"

"Of course. Well, get a move on," snapped Algy as he left the room.

Biggles had barely finished dressing when a boy arrived with half a dozen cards on a tray, and the information that the gentlemen who had tendered them were waiting below. He hurried along the corridor to Algy's room and opened the door. "Buck up," he said, "or we shall never get out; the first of the storm-troops are below."

"The who?"

Biggles cast a casual eye over the slips of paste-board in his hand. "H. F. Carruthers, 12th Bengalis," he read.

"Looks like a lad looking for a free flip home. J. L. Browner, *Bombay Argus*; F. L. Winters, *West Indian Photographic Agency*; Sirdar Ali Sha—wonder what he wants?"

"Tell 'em all there's nothing doing," said Algy bluntly, picking up his bag.

"I have," replied Biggles simply, "or at least, I've told the boy to tell 'em."

A sound of voices, coming along the corridor, reached their ears, and the next moment the door was pushed open and an athletic young man entered, followed by a protesting native servant.

"Listen, chaps," began the young man apologetically; "I'm Carruthers of the 12th. I sent my card up. I've got three months' leave, starting today, and I'm full out to get home as quickly as possible——"

"Then you'd better go by Imperial Airways; we aren't leaving for a fortnight yet."

The subaltern's face fell. "Oh!" he groaned. "The paper said——"

"Yes, I know it did, but the paper knows nothing about it. Sorry."

"So am I," confessed the crestfallen officer. "Cheerio; sorry to have butted in."

"Don't mention it," returned Biggles, and then, turning to Algy, "Come on, laddie; let's hoof it or we shall be pestered to death."

"Pardon, gentlemen!"

Both pilots swung round as the words reached them from the direction of the door; they found themselves looking into the sombre face of a heavily moustached man carrying a fur coat over his arm. "I beg your pardon for this intrusion," he went on, "which only circumstances of extreme urgency could warrant. May I present myself; my name is Sirdar Ali Sha."

"I'm sorry, sir, but if you are looking for a joy-ride I'm afraid there's nothing doing," interrupted Biggles. "We are leaving in a few minutes for Gwadir, on our way to England."

"That is what I understand," nodded their visitor imperturbably. "I believe you are going via Persia and the Black Sea ports?"

"That is our intention."

"May I ask if you have the authority of the Persian Government to fly over its territory?"

Biggles started. "No, we haven't," he confessed, "but we do not anticipate any difficulty. Most National Aero Clubs extend their courtesy to foreign pilots."

"That may be so, but there are exceptions. It so happens that I have received an urgent message, a very urgent message, demanding my immediate presence in Teheran. I noticed the paragraph in the paper this morning and have called to see if we could reach an agreement. I am quite willing to pay any reasonable sum for my passage, and in addition I could furnish you with documents that might make your welcome in Persia—and Russia—more sincere than it might otherwise be. I would also mention that I am not a stranger to the air."

Biggles hesitated. "Well," he said, "we don't normally take passengers, and, frankly, I don't feel like establishing a precedent. After all, although we do not anticipate any trouble, accidents do happen, and should such a calamity occur we should feel morally responsible for any injury that you might suffer."

A shadow flitted across the heavy face of their visitor, and he looked at the two pilots for a moment, searchingly, before he replied. "Of course," he said slowly. "Still, you are both experienced pilots and I am quite willing to take the risk. In fact, I am willing to give you a letter completely exonerating you from blame in case anything untoward should occur."

Again Biggles hesitated. "All right," he said slowly at last; "if my partner agrees, and provided we can arrive at a financial understanding, I will take you. But I must make it quite clear that you come at your own risk and that I cannot definitely guarantee time of arrival."

"That is understood, of course," agreed the other. "What time do we start?"

Biggles glanced at his watch. "It is now eight-thirty," he said. "Suppose we say we will leave the ground at nine-thirty—will that suit you?"

"Admirably."

"Have you any luggage?"

"Only an attaché-case."

"All right, then. We will meet at nine-twenty on the aerodrome and leave the ground at nine-thirty. Our first stop will be Gwadir and then Lingeh."

III

The sun was blazing with the full power of its afternoon heat as the "Vandal" forged its way through the shimmering haze that hung above the Persian Gulf, a haze that turned both sea and sky to the colour of burnished steel. The horizon existed in imagination only; the gradual darkening of the sky just below the nose of the engine showed vaguely where the sky ended and the sea began.

Biggles studied his instrument-board diligently, from time to time glancing ahead as if expecting some landmark to show up through the haze. He had followed the coastline of Persia as far as Jask, and then cut across the strait of Ormuz, actually passing over that spur of Arabia called Oman, on a straight course for Lingeh, which, according to his reckoning, now lay some fifty miles ahead. A dark-brown blot loomed up through the haze, slightly to his left; it lay across the water like a monster that had risen from the depths of the ocean and lay basking on the surface. He nudged Algy and then pointed with the forefinger of his left hand to an insignificant speck on the map which bore the name Tumb Island. At the same moment the steady rhythm of the engines changed slightly, but it was sufficient to bring Smyth's head to the low doorway leading from the cabin.

Biggles's eyes sought his rev. counters and rested on the wavering needles of the instruments. The engine revs. had fallen, and were still falling. Simultaneously the nose of the machine turned until it pointed directly towards the island. The roar of the engines died away suddenly, burst into life again, and then faded away to a gentle purr. The nose of the amphibian tilted down, and a few minutes later the keel cut a long white scar across the smooth water of a natural harbour that yawned invitingly in the sandy beach.

As the machine ran to a standstill Algy looked at Biggles with wide-open eyes. "What's wrong?" he said.

"Dunno," replied Biggles laconically as the keel grated gently on the shelving beach. He climbed out of his seat and slipped down into the shallow water. The door in the hull opened, and Smyth and their passenger stepped out.

"That outlet-pipe clogged again, sir, I reckon," observed Smyth.

Biggles nodded. "I think so," he said. "It's nothing very serious, anyway, but I thought it was safer to try and put it right here rather than risk the next fifty miles or so of open sea to the mainland." The last sentence he addressed to his passenger, who had lighted a cigar and was surveying the unpromising coast-line of the island with disgust.

"Quite right," was the quick reply; "safety first. I suppose you will soon be able to put things right?"

"Oh, yes, I think so," replied Biggles casually. "We'll get to work on her as soon as we can, and this time we'll make sure we clear the outlet thoroughly—it seems as if there's some sediment in one of the tanks."

"I hope it's nothing very serious," observed the other. "We might have to wait here for a long time before we were picked up; after all, we can't drain the tanks."

"We always carry a good stock of provisions, so I don't think we need worry on that score."

"Maybe not, but you will please remember that my mission is an urgent one, so I trust you will lose no time in clearing out the obstruction."

"Quite," replied Biggles vaguely.

But the sun was sinking like a ball of fire in the west before Biggles was sure that no foreign matter remained to obstruct the flow of petrol.

"It will be dark in five minutes, so I am afraid it isn't worth taking a chance to get to Lingeh tonight," said Biggles in a tone of disappointment. "It's only a small place and we might easily miss it. I suggest we make ourselves as comfortable as we can for the night, and push on in the morning. Get some of those cases out of the cabin, Smyth; we shall need some food, anyway. I think that little group of palms a bit lower down will be the best spot for camp."

So slowly as to be hardly noticeable, the moon lost its brilliancy. The pale flickering fingers of another day felt searchingly in the Eastern sky and shed a grey, mysterious light over the sea and the barren sandy island with its group of stunted palms. The rim of the sun showed above the horizon; a shaft of light fell upon the gently stirring palm-fronds, and upon the recumbent figure of a man, wrapped in a fur coat, who lay upon the sand.

As the sun's rays reached his eyes, he awoke, yawned, and then sat up, stretching. He glanced around. A faint sound rising and falling on the breeze above the steady beat of the surf upon the shore brought him to his feet in a single bound, as if impelled by an invisible spring. He flashed a glance along the beach and then turned in the direction of the sound, his face working curiously as his eyes picked out a tiny moving speck afar off, a speck that vanished even as he watched it. For a long time he stood staring, long after the sound of the aero-engines had faded into silence.

A cold fury smouldered in his eyes as he turned towards the packing-cases, which remained as they had been placed the previous evening. On the largest, held in place by a stone, lay an envelope, and he reached for it with a slow movement that was deadly in its deliberation. His nostrils quivered as he read the superscription:

Ivan Nikitoff, Esq.,
Tumb Island,
Nr. Persia.

With hands that trembled slightly, he tore the envelope open, took out the single sheet of paper that it contained, and read:

Dear Ivan,

I find I shall not be going your way, after all. Everything you will be likely to require (except our society) for the next three weeks will be found in the cases. In case the time hangs heavily on your hands, you will find a book in the case marked Number 1, *which may afford you some relief.*

Yours in haste,
JAMES BIGGLESWORTH.

"The thing that beats me is how you knew about that message he received, calling him to Teheran," muttered Algy, when, late in the day, the "Vandal" ran to a standstill near the Bund at Basra, and Biggles had made certain called-for explanations.

"For the simple reason that I sent it," replied Biggles carelessly. "At least, it was arranged by me in collaboration with certain people who shall be nameless that he should receive such a message."

"But, good heavens, surely such a letter would be in a secret code, if it was genuine?"

"It was—but do you suppose our people don't know the code?"

"But what's going to happen to Ivan?"

"I fixed the whole thing up with Pat. All we did was to shove that paragraph in the paper, send the message in his own code, and hope he'd rise to the bait. Well, he did. It will so happen that a sloop will be passing the island in about three weeks, which by a curious coincidence will be just about the time that Pat's business is concluded."

"You seem to have thought it well out," observed Algy. "By the way, what was the name of the book you left him?" he asked curiously.

Biggles paused in the act of taking off his helmet, and a slow smile spread over his face. "*Three Weeks*," he said. "I hope he'll see the point."

CHAPTER II

THE SHEIKH AND THE GREEK

BIGGLES reflectively sipped an ice-cold cordial outside a restaurant in the Avenue el Fontana in Alexandria.

"There is one thing I should like to do before we leave Alex.," he told Algy confidentially, "and that is, find out what sort of a price we are likely to get for our pearls. I seem to remember that Egypt is supposed to be a good market for them. We might do better in Paris, but we should probably get stung badly by the Customs people there, or before we get there. The Italians at Benghazi might even have something to say about them. We should stand a better chance here of disposing of them quietly; anyway, they are a bit of an anxiety and the sooner we turn them into hard cash the better."

"I agree," returned Algy promptly. "There's a jeweller's across the way—why not stroll over? Don't let him see them all or he'll try to beat you down. Show him one first."

"That's not a bad idea," replied Biggles, taking a small washleather bag from his breast pocket. He untied the string, inserted his forefinger and thumb and took out one of the two large pink pearls presented to them by Li Chi.

"I shouldn't show him that one," said Algy quickly. "Keep the pair together; they will be worth far more as a pair than separate."

Biggles nodded. "Yes——" he began, but broke off with an ejaculation as the stone slipped from his fingers, bounced off his shoe, and rolled along the pavement, coming to rest at the feet of a good-looking, immaculately dressed man who sat at a table a little lower down. The owner of the feet stooped quickly, picked it up, and after an appraising glance returned it to its anxious owner with a courteous bow.

"Many thanks," said Biggles, relieved.

"A pretty toy," observed the man suavely, speaking with a slight foreign accent, and then, "It seemed to know where to come," he added with a significant smile.

Biggles hesitated. "How do you mean?" he said curiously.

The stranger lifted his palms in the Semitic gesture peculiar to the Middle East. "I am a buyer of such luxuries," he said in a low voice. "If at any time the one I have seen is for disposal I hope I may have the honour of being allowed to acquire it."

"Sorry, but that one is not for sale," replied Biggles, suspiciously, "but if you care to sit down—I have others——"

He tilted the pearls they had recovered from the Kaisiora into his palm. "How about these?"

The stranger shrugged his shoulders and pursed his lips in a disparaging smile. "They are merely pearls," he said softly, "but——" He broke off with a foreign exclamation and stared at the second pink pearl, which Biggles had placed beside the first. He drew in his breath with a sibilant hiss. "You have another," he muttered quickly, raising his eyes to Biggles's face.

The pilot dropped the two pink pearls into the bag and replaced it in his pocket. "Yes," he said slowly; "they'd make a nice pair of ear-rings for a princess. Suppose they were for sale, how much would they be worth?" he asked casually.

"A much larger sum than I have at my disposal here," admitted the stranger readily. "I do not buy for myself——" He dropped his voice to a whisper. "I am an agent for the illustrious Sheikh Abd-el-Ahmud, who has the most magnificent collection in Arabia. He must see them to decide a value, and the price will be a fair one, I assure you; far better than you will get from the bandits of Alexandria or Cairo who call themselves pearl-dealers."

"Where is the Sheikh?" asked Biggles, becoming interested.

"At his palace in Hejaz—on the east coast of the Red Sea," replied the other.

"My eye! That settles it; we can't trail all the way down to the Red Sea," said Biggles decisively.

"But why not? I promise you the difference you will receive in price will more than recompense you for the trouble. Besides, the Sheikh is famous for his hospitality——"

"Never mind that," broke in Biggles coldly; "we're talking about pearls. How far is this place?"

"Five hundred miles, perhaps less, but I have a fast boat."

"I have an aeroplane, if it comes to that," observed Biggles, thinking quickly.

The stranger started, and his eyes flashed suddenly. "An aeroplane," he repeated slowly.

Biggles nodded. "Look here," he said; "let us think it over. We don't know you and you don't know us, but if you can assure us that we should receive a fair price—a price that might tempt me to part with them—we might consider it. By the way, how should we be paid?" he asked curiously.

"Why, in gold, surely," replied the other quickly. "Such men as my patron do not use paper money. The Sheikh is rich far beyond the Western ideas of wealth," he added.

"All right. You think things over; we'll do the same and meet you here this evening to let you know what we've decided," said Biggles, rising.

The stranger took a card from a gold case and handed it to the pilot with a little bow. "Thank you," he said. "I will await your pleasure," and raising his hat he walked quickly away.

"Well, what do you think of him?" asked Biggles, when he was out of earshot.

"It's hard to say," replied Algy. "What nationality is he, do you think?"

"Goodness only knows. Eurasian, I imagine; possibly a Greek or Armenian Jew." He looked at the card in his hand. "Constantine Stampoulos," he read aloud. "Well, that's Greek enough, but I have a deep-rooted suspicion of the type, although he certainly looked affluent. He may be right about the Sheikh paying a good price for the pearls. All the lads along the Red Sea coast are enthusiastic collectors of pearls, I've been told. The best stuff from the Persian Gulf goes there, or to India, to say nothing of those they find themselves in the Red Sea. Let's get some lunch and talk it over."

II

Biggles leaned back in his seat and from five thousand feet surveyed the glorious panorama below with silent approval. He was heading south for Heliopolis, one hundred and twenty-five miles away, where he proposed to refuel before going to El Tuara, the oasis in which the Sheikh's palace was situated. Below lay the delta of the Nile, with its innumerable villages, stretching like an open-work lace design to the blue Mediterranean now far behind them. Ahead, clear-cut in the crystal atmosphere, were the minarets of the Citadel Mosque in Cairo, and the Mokattam Hills.

It was the morning following their meeting with Stampoulos. He had readily agreed to make the journey by air; in fact, he had forestalled Biggles by suggesting it, almost at once, when they had met in the evening as arranged. He had assured them it would be possible to land either on the waters of a bay near the palace or on the open *sabkha*, which extended for miles around it.

The airmen, after a brief consultation, confident of their

ability to guard their own interests, had decided to make the expedition. Details had been quickly arranged, with the result that the Greek was now seated in the cabin with Smyth, no doubt enjoying the wonderful vista below.

After a brief pause at Heliopolis to refuel, where Algy had changed places with Stampoulos in order that the Greek might guide the pilot to their destination, they were soon in the air again on a more easterly course, which would take them down the west coast of Arabia. The Red Sea soon lay below, and as the machine sped onwards Biggles eyed the arid desolation under his left wing with mixed feelings, wondering if they had been wise in accompanying a stranger to a spot so remote from civilization.

He derived some comfort from the activity on the sea, where, from time to time, tiny black destroyers ploughed long white furrows in the blue as they kept unceasing watch over the vital and coveted strip of water that terminated in the Suez Canal.

For more than three hours they flew along a barren coast, over deep wadis and rocky hills, behind which the desert, the dreaded, uncrossed Rub al Khali, rolled back until it merged into the purple haze of the far distance. Once or twice they saw the camels of an ancient caravanserai winding slowly northwards to the markets of Egypt over trails that were old when Moses led the Children of Israel out of the land of the Pharaohs.

Suddenly Stampoulos nudged the pilot and pointed with outstretched finger towards a grove of tall date-palms, in the centre of which stood a fort-like building crowned by two squat towers. It was nearly a mile from the end of a deep incision in the coastline, and as Biggles throttled back he passed a critical eye over the surroundings. Nevertheless, it was not until he was within a few hundred feet of the ground that he noticed a brown-painted dhow, moored close to the rocks, so perfectly did it blend with the background. He circled once over the palm-grove, and then, dropping his wheels, landed bumpily on a large flat area of gravelly earth a short distance away.

"I will leave you to do what is necessary to the machine while I tell the Emir of our coming," said Stampoulos, hurrying in the direction of the palace, which they now saw in the middle of a group of low Arab dwellings.

They taxied the machine into the shade of a palm, and, leaving Smyth in charge, followed the path taken by the Greek. They reached a pointed Moorish archway, around which loitered several Wahhabi Arabs, armed with long rifles and formidable curved knives. The Arabs stared at them sullenly as they passed between them into a small courtyard, on the opposite side of which was the main entrance to the palace. It presented a rather squalid appearance and was hardly what they had expected.

The Sheikh, who broke off what seemed to be a heated conversation with Stampoulos when he saw them approaching, was waiting to receive them, and his manner and appearance were even less prepossessing than his palace. He was wearing a dirty white robe, over which was thrown a striped *haik* woven in a pattern of alternate black and red bars, fringed with curious cabalistic-like figures in the corner.

Biggles found himself looking into a pair of dark challenging eyes set in a brown face. He sensed at once a hostile atmosphere, which a forced smile did not allay, but in answer to the Sheikh's "*Allah hadik*" he bowed gravely and turned to the Greek expectantly.

"The Sheikh is anxious to start on a journey," said Stampoulos apologetically, "so will you show him the pearls at once?"

Biggles laid the pearls on a low table between them, and the Sheikh examined them greedily, muttering something to the Greek in a language the pilot did not understand.

"He says he will pay one thousand pounds for them," said Stampoulos.

"One thousand pounds!" cried Biggles incredulously. "They are worth three times that sum in the open market."

Again the Greek spoke to the Sheikh.

"He says they are not a good colour; he will not pay more," translated the Greek.

"Give me the pearls," said Biggles sternly; "we are wasting our time."

Stampoulos interpreted the message. The Sheikh picked up the bag, which Biggles had laid on the table, replaced the pearls, and handed it to him without a word.

"One moment before you go," said Stampoulos quickly, as Biggles dropped the bag into his pocket after feeling it surreptitiously to make sure the pearls were in it. "I am sorry this deal has fallen through, but"—he shrugged his shoulders—"the Emir is not well disposed today. He is anxious to be off on his journey and he asks me if you will consider taking him in your machine."

"No, I will not," replied Biggles shortly.

The Sheikh, who seemed to await his decision anxiously, appeared to understand he had replied in the negative and said something quickly to the Greek.

"He says he will pay you two hundred and fifty pounds if you will take him to Azir," said Stampoulos.

"Where's that?"

"A small port on the opposite coast."

For a moment Biggles was spellbound, tempted to agree, for the offer was as munificent as the other was niggardly, but his temper got the upper hand. "No," he almost snapped. "Come on, we can just get back before dark."

"No! I shall stay here now I am here," returned Stampoulos coolly.

"It looks to me as if you've had a cheap trip," sneered Biggles, with a sudden suspicion darting into his mind. He turned on his heel and with a brief, "Come on, Algy," stalked furiously out of the palace, certain that in some way or other he had been exploited by the Greek. He climbed into his seat and took off without a word.

They had been in the air about twenty minutes when he relinquished control to Algy and took something from his pocket. The next instant he had snatched the control-column from his partner's hand and was sideslipping steeply towards one of the many small islands that cluster along the coast, dropping on to the water on the lee side of one of them.

"Great Scott, what's wrong?" cried Algy in bewilderment, staring at Biggles's face, which had turned as white as chalk and out of which his eyes blazed like live coals.

"Wrong!" snarled Biggles. "That crooked double-crossing dago has done us."

"Done us! How?" exclaimed Algy aghast.

In answer Biggles held out his hand, on the palm of which rested two pearls. They were about the size of the pink pearls, but they were dull and lifeless. They were, in fact, "dead" pearls, such as are sometimes found in molluscs.

Algy's eyes narrowed. "Heck! That was slick," he breathed. "What are we going to do?"

"Do? I'm going back," said Biggles harshly. "They're not getting away with that."

"But we can't tackle that bunch of cut-throats single-handed. Hullo—what's all this——?" he broke off, staring over Biggles's shoulder.

A drab destroyer was bearing down on them at full speed, two white ostrich-plumes of spray leaping up from the knife-like bow. While still a hundred yards away it swung hard over and then churned up a whirlpool of foam as it went aback. Almost before it had stopped a small boat had dropped from the davits and was skimming towards them under the swift strokes of half a dozen pairs of oars; an officer sat in the stern.

"Who are you?" he said curtly, as the boat ran alongside.

Biggles frowned. "I'll give you two guesses," he said. "Who are you anyway?"

"H.M.S. *Scud.* Captain Watkins wants a word with

you. Bring your papers—step along, please," was the peremptory reply.

"Who are you ordering about?"

"You," snapped the Lieutenant. "Step lively, now, unless you want to be blown out of the water."

Biggles swallowed hard. Quivering with rage, he put his log-book in his pocket, jumped into the boat, and a moment later scrambled up the ladder that had been lowered to receive them. He flushed as two blue-jackets fell in, one on either side of him, and marched him briskly to where the Captain awaited him.

"Your name?" said the Captain coldly, holding out his hand for the "Vandal's" log.

"Biggleswörth," replied Biggles icily.

The Captain started. "No relation, by any chance, to a fellow who served in 266 Squadron during the war, are you?"

Biggles nodded. "I was in 266," he said wonderingly.

"Good heavens! My young brother was with you. He told me a lot about you before he was——"

Biggles stared and then thawed. "Watkins—of course," he mused. "A good lad," he went on. "We called him the Professor. Lacey—who is with me now—the Professor and I did many shows together. We were with him when he went—west."

Captain Watkins rose and extended his hand. "Pleased to meet you," he smiled; "but what are you doing here? Don't you know that this is a prohibited area?"

Biggles's eyes opened wide. "I'm dashed if I did," he admitted, and forthwith related briefly what had happened from the moment they had met Stampoulos in Alexandria.

The Captain exchanged a quick glance with the Lieutenant, who had entered the room. "Sounds a grim business to me," he observed. "Tell me, what was he like, this Stampoulos?"

Biggles described him, and again the eyes of the Captain sought those of the second-in-command.

"And this Sheikh—what did you say his name was, Abd-el-Ahmud—what was *he* like?"

Again the pilot drew a rough description, and the Captain pursed his lips. "I wonder," he said softly, "I wonder." He unlocked a safe, took out a docket, and selected a photograph. Covering the top part of the head and the body with his finger and thumb, he beckoned to the pilot. "Was he anything like that?" he asked.

"That's the man," began Biggles, but broke off with a gasp of amazement as the Captain lifted his hand and exposed the rest of the picture. It was a well-dressed middle-aged man in European clothes. "Who is he?" he asked.

"He has many names," replied Watkins, "but his real one is Lafoix, René Lafoix; our people got this snap of him in Paris. He came out here about twenty years ago as a French secret-service agent. He still works for the French, of course, but he has developed some profitable sidelines in pearls, slaves and hashish. Stampoulos, by the way, is his agent in Alexandria. We've had Lafoix in our hands a dozen times, but he's slipped through our fingers; an eel is a roll of sandpaper compared with him.

The trouble is he's played the Arab so long that he *is* one. When we catch him he's got an honest-to-goodness load of hides on board; when we nab his dhows with dope or slaves he isn't there. It isn't that which annoys us as much as his infernal nerve in writing a book about it, saying how he's fooled us. It made France rock with mirth. Our people said nothing to France about it, but they said something to *us* about it, believe me. We've got to get him, and when we do we'll see who laughs last and longest.

"We're watching for him now," he went on quickly. "We know he's along the coast here somewhere, waiting for a chance to slip up to Greece for another load of dope; it all comes from there. To get it to Egypt, where it is as much in demand as tobacco at home, he ships it to Syria, brings it overland by camel to the coast hereabouts, and then rushes it across the ditch in dhows, which come back with a load of slaves. The dope disappears; broken up into small parcels, it gets into Cairo a thousand different ways. You see, the trouble is, even if we do nab him going north, he'll only laugh at us, because he'll have a clean bill of lading. But when we spot him this time we shall never take our eyes off him again, and he knows it."

"He's got a dhow there now," interrupted Biggles, "but he wanted me to fly him to Azir."

"He did? I begin to see the drift of this. Stampoulos got wind that we were watching and came down here to warn him. I'll bet you any money the Greek knew all about your aircraft before you spoke to him; the pearl business was only an excuse to get in touch with you.

He knew he couldn't get down here any other way through the net we've drawn about the place. They then got the idea of flying out of it—pretty good. They've got spies everywhere. Every Arab on both sides of the water is in with them. What are you going to do about your pearls?"

"I was just wondering," replied Biggles slowly. "Have you got a machine-gun on board?"

"But you can't go and shoot them up! It would start another European war——"

"I wasn't thinking of anything so crude," broke in Biggles, "but if you'll help me to get my pearls I'll help you get his body. Listen——"

III

Biggles landed the "Vandal" near the grove of date-palms, handed the controls to Algy, and jumped lightly to the ground. The engine roared again and the machine soared up into the blue.

He made his way quickly towards the trees, and ignoring a scowling group of Arabs strode up to the entrance of the palace. "Are you there, Stampoulos?" he called loudly. A dozen Arabs began to edge towards him, but paused as they looked into the muzzle of a revolver.

Stampoulos entered, dressed in Arab clothes. "What do you want?" he said, his eyes glinting evilly.

"In the first place, my pearls," replied Biggles, replacing his revolver and lighting a cigarette.

"Is that all?" sneered the Greek.

"All for the moment," replied Biggles coolly. "Where's the Sheikh? I've a proposal to make—ah, there he is! Now, listen, Stampoulos," he went on; "translate as I go. I don't like the company I'm in, and the sooner I'm out of it the better I shall be pleased. You've got my pearls, and you were pretty smart, I'll admit. You give them back to me—no, wait a minute, I haven't finished—give me my pearls plus one hundred pounds, gold, and I'll fly you and your Sheikh to Azir right away."

The Greek laughed, a short, unpleasant laugh.

"Do you think you are in a position to dictate terms?" he scoffed.

"I certainly do, or, not being entirely a fool, I should not have returned to this den of thieves."

"What is to prevent me killing you now?" asked the Greek, with an evil smile.

"Come here and I'll show you," said Biggles, imperturbably, crossing to the window. The other followed. "I'm going to show you what will happen if I'm not back in my machine in half an hour," he went on, waving his handkerchief through the window.

The "Vandal", circling above, swept down in a steep dive near the palm-grove. A sheet of orange flame leapt upwards and a deafening detonation shook the palace to its foundations. The "Vandal" made a quick stalling turn and Smyth could be seen crouching low over a Vickers gun.

Rat-tat-tat-tat-tat-tat. Rat-tat-tat-tat-tat—— The sand flew up in a long line as the mechanic put half a belt of ammunition into the ground as the machine roared past.

Biggles saw the Arabs running for cover. "My friends have had quite a lot of experience at this sort of thing," he observed casually, "and if anything happens to me I can promise you that neither this building nor any man on the oasis will be standing by the time they've finished. The dhow in the offing will also make a handy target. Furthermore," he bluffed as an afterthought, "I have told them if they want any assistance to call up R.A.F. machines by radio from Aden and Khartoum. Every gunboat within five hundred miles will pick up the call and hurry along to see what it's all about."

"Where did you get that gun?" snarled the Greek, with an evil scowl; "it wasn't——"

"Bosh!" snapped Biggles. "Do you think we show passengers all our equipment? Well, what are you going to do about it?"

The mention of the Royal Air Force and the gunboats seemed to shake the Greek, for his face turned a pale olive-green, and he spoke rapidly to the Sheikh for some minutes.

"Very good," he said at the end; "we accept your terms. When would you be ready to go?"

"Now," replied Biggles. "It will be dark before we get there if you don't look sharp. Put the pearls on this table and count out the money, and I'll give you my word that I'll fly you direct to Azir without any further conditions or argument. Make yourselves look respectable—if you can. I don't want any questions from the authorities if they happen to be about."

"Nor I," said the Greek involuntarily.

"I thought you wouldn't," agreed Biggles. "Well. come on, let's be moving."

Two hours later, Biggles, with the pearls reposing in his breastpocket and a bag containing one hundred sovereigns on the seat beside him, peered ahead into the glare of the setting sun for the coastline of Egypt. He turned a little to the north as it came into view and shortly afterwards picked out the white domes and minarets of the mosque at Azir. He saw something else, too, something that brought a faint smile to the corners of his mouth. A small rakish destroyer lay alongside the ramshackle pier.

He throttled back, landed on the water, taxied quickly towards the pier and switched off. A buzz of conversation came from the cabin. "What's the matter?" he asked, as he ducked through the low doorway.

"Why is the British destroyer here?" asked the Greek venomously.

"They know best," replied Biggles vaguely. "Why, you've nothing to worry about, have you?"

"No, but they may ask questions," protested Stampoulos, uncomfortably.

"Well, I can't help that," replied Biggles gravely. "We've got to go ashore, because I have no more petrol. If they ask anybody questions, it will be us, not you, and our papers are all in order," he went on. "But to be on the safe side we had better say you are our servants. That will sound reasonable enough—eh, what do you think?"

"A good idea," cried the Greek quickly.

"All right; we'll go first, and you follow with our suitcases; here are the keys."

An obsequious Egyptian was waiting for them at the mud-built office at the end of the pier.

"Anything to declare, *effendi*?" he asked, with an ingratiating smile.

"Nothing," replied Biggles, and walked on.

The Sheikh and the Greek were about to pass with the suitcases when an officer in white ducks, with two bluejackets in attendance, stepped out of the office.

"Anything in those bags?" he asked casually.

"Nothing," replied the Greek, inserting a key and throwing back the lid of the suitcase he carried, with a mocking bow. Look," he said, with a theatrical wave of his hand and a smile that held a sneer he could not conceal. The smile died on his lips as he followed the officer's eyes to the suitcase. He stared, and his jaw sagged foolishly.

The suitcase was packed solid with a dark substance, from which arose a faint but peculiar aroma.

"Nothing, did you say?" exclaimed Watkins incredulously. "Fifty pounds of hashish seems to me to be something—catch him!"

The Sheikh, after one fleeting glance at the contents of the case, leapt at Biggles like a tiger, a knife in his hand, but a bluejacket tripped him up and he crashed headlong. Half a dozen sailors poured out of the office and threw themselves on him.

Stampoulos could only stand and stare at the contents of the second suitcase, which had revealed another load of the narcotic. He seemed to be dazed, and followed the sailors unresistingly.

"Got your pearls, Bigglesworth?" asked Watkins, smiling.

"Yes, and you've got the body," grinned Biggles. "Empty that dope of yours out of our suitcases; we want to be getting along. See you later."

CHAPTER 12

YELLOW FREIGHT

WITH his goggles swinging lightly from the finger of his left hand, Biggles, with Algy at his side, walked slowly along the tarmac of the sun-scorched aerodrome at Heliopolis to where the "Vandal," with Smyth standing by the propeller, rested in the shade of a hangar, in readiness for the trip to Benghazi, the next port of call on their homeward journey.

Before they reached the machine, however, their attention was attracted to a mechanic hurrying towards them.

"Looking for us, or I'm a Dutchman," observed Biggles curiously. "I wonder what he wants?"

"Beg pardon, sir, but will you please have a word with Colonel Grivin; he's waiting in the office."

"What office?"

"The Nile and North African Aviation Company, sir."

Biggles raised his eyebrows. "Lead on; we'll follow," he said.

A tall, spare, grey-haired man with a troubled face rose to meet them as they entered the offices of the well-known Egyptian operating company.

"Come in, Bigglesworth, come in," he said tersely, leading the way to an inner office. "Pleased to meet you," he went on quickly when they were seated. "I heard a lot about you during the war; I was at Wing H.Q. when you were in 266 Squadron."

Biggles nodded. "Yes, I remember your name now, sir. Can I do something for you?"

Colonel Grivin drummed nervously on his desk for a moment before replying. "I don't know," he muttered anxiously. "It's difficult—very difficult. The fact is, I'm in a jam, and I'm just about at my wits' end." He leaned forward suddenly. "You had a pretty good record in the war, Biggleswortth; you seemed to have a knack of—er—sorting things out. I want you to think this over. When I've finished you can either stand by me or you can walk out of that door, and I shan't say a word. Did you know Trevor Dawlish?"

"I've heard of him, but I don't remember ever meeting him. He used to be in 56, didn't he?"

"He was. Until a short time ago he was my best pilot. He left here a month ago for Benghazi, on a trip to Paris, with a special freight. He never got there. Service machines found his crash a fortnight ago in the mountains, near El Farosha, about four miles the other side of Karouma, which is the first emergency landing-ground on the run. He was—well, it was a heck of a crash—burnt out."

The Colonel paused for a moment before continuing.

"Three days ago Bert Makins, another of my pilots, headed east on the same trip, also with freight. It seems as if he tried to get in at Karouma but made a mess of it. He finished up by crashing into the rocks on the north side of the landing-ground, and was burnt up before he could get out."

"Bad show."

The Colonel's jaw set grimly. "It's worse than that, Bigglesworth," he said in a strained voice. "Poor Trevor and Bert were murdered."

The two pilots stared at the speaker aghast.

"Murdered? What are you talking about?" stammered Biggles.

Colonel Grivin crossed the room in swift silent strides and flung the door open. A red-fezzed native whom Biggles recognized as the petrol *effendi* who had just helped him fill the "Vandal's" tanks was leaning against a wall in the passage.

"What do you want?" barked the Colonel. "What are you hanging about here for?"

"*Baksheesh*," muttered the man sheepishly.

"Well, get out of it," snarled the Colonel. He watched the man out of sight and then returned to his visitors, mopping his face with a large handkerchief. "What was I saying?" he muttered absently.

"You said something about Dawlish and Makins being murdered," Biggles reminded him.

"They were. They were murdered for the freight they had on board."

Biggles raised his eyebrows.

"Gold," said the Colonel, in a curiously quiet voice. "We are shipping gold from here to Paris. I've got a contract that will make the firm—or I had. The quickly changing price of bullion makes every moment it spends *en route* important. These consignments are British, but we are only taking them as far as Paris. We fly them through this sector. The first one or two lots went through without trouble. Then Dawlish cracked up. I had to call in Service machines to find him, but what they didn't know, what nobody knew except me, was the nature of the cargo. When we got to the wreck it had gone. I suspected foul play at once and I told Bert so—he was due to take the next lot through. He only laughed, but he knew well enough that it was true, that someone had got on the trail of the metal. Well, they got him too, and the gold he was carrying. But how? Why did he try to land at Karouma; that's what I want to know. How did the crooks force him down?"

"Someone tinkering with the machines at this end," suggested Algy.

"That's what I thought at first, naturally, but in that case how could they know that the machine wouldn't crack up taking off here? How could they time the crash at the only emergency landing-ground between here and Matruh, which is the last English-speaking petrol-station between here and Tripoli? Well, I'm going to get the swine who killed those two boys, if I spend the rest of my life doing it. I only wish I could fly myself, but I can't. And I've got another consignment to go through today."

"But you've more pilots and machines?"

"Yes, but who on earth is going to fly to certain death? I've two pilots left. Thomson is one, but he's down with fever, or, maybe, he'd go. Lorne is the other, and he's dug his toes in. He says he's a married man and is willing to fly anything anywhere—except gold. He has refused to fly any machine if an ounce of metal is put on board. That's what he says, and he means it, and I can't blame him."

"What do you expect me to do?" asked Biggles quietly.

"I'm asking you to take this consignment through," said Colonel Grivin simply. "If it doesn't go, the Company's broke, busted wide open, and that's that. Apart from that, if there is any man I know who might get to the bottom of what's going on, it's you."

"You mean you want us to take it in *our* machine?"

"In yours, or one of mine; I don't care which. There are three machines for you to choose from in the sheds. They're all enclosed-cabin types. I can't offer you anything big to make on the job, because I haven't got it, but I'll make it worth your while. I am willing to give all I've got to keep up the reputation of the firm, which is an all-British show, and in trying to find out who killed those two lads."

"I understand," said Biggles. "Do you mind if I talk this over for a few minutes with the others? Give me, say, half an hour, then I'll let you have a decision. By the way, has any particular machine been booked for this particular trip?"

"Yes, there she is; they are just bringing her out of the sheds," replied the Colonel, pointing to a single-engined cabin-monoplane, which was being slowly drawn out of the firm's hangar.

"Thanks," returned Biggles. Outside he settled himself down in the shade of the office and cupped his chin in his hands.

"Well, what do you make——?" began Algy.

"Don't talk for a minute; let me think," Biggles told him.

A quarter of an hour passed in silence; then he rose to his feet and walked slowly across to the aircraft that now stood on the tarmac in readiness for the flight. He stared at it for a long time, studying it closely from several angles He climbed into the cockpit, examined the control-column, instruments, and short-wave wireless equipment. Then he closed the door, took up the small piece of matting and studied the floor of the cockpit intently. He climbed down from the machine still deep in thought and a trifle pale.

"I'm going to fly this machine," he announced harshly.

"You mean 'we'," corrected Algy.

"I said I," replied Biggles firmly. "You're going to stand by here with the 'Vandal', with Smyth and the Colonel. Don't argue," he concluded shortly, turning towards the Company's offices.

"I'm going to fly your machine," he told the Colonel. "Where's the gold?"

"In my safe."

"Good. Keep it there. Make up some more packets to look like it and have it put aboard when I'm ready. The best thing would be to knock up some scrap lead to give it weight. Stand by with the real stuff, ready to slip it into the 'Vandal' when I give the word. How far away is this place, Karouma?"

"About an hour's run."

"Who's in command of the R.A.F. units here?"

"Bruton—Group-Captain."

"Do you know him?"

"Quite well."

"Good; let's go across. I want you to introduce me to him. I may want some assistance if what I have in mind comes off. And, Algy, I want you to slip into Cairo as quickly as you can in the Colonel's car and do a bit of shopping for me."

"What do you want?"

"A pair of white mice in a small cage."

Algy stared at him incredulously, and then a look of understanding slowly dawned in his eyes. "Great Scott!" he breathed. "So that's it."

"That's how I figure it," replied Biggles shortly. "There are still some things I don't quite understand—but I soon shall," he added grimly. "Come on, Colonel; let's go down to the Station Headquarters."

II

The blueness of the Mediterranean is proverbial, but seen from five thousand feet, with depths varying from the shallows near the beach to the deeper water farther from the land, the riot of colour is indescribable. Every shade of green, blue, and purple is represented, according to the depth and the nature of the sea-bed.

But Biggles was too engrossed in other matters to enjoy the beauties of nature; his eyes only left the small cage suspended from his instrument-board to probe the surrounding sky. Every nerve was tense, for he was waiting—waiting for something to happen. Just what that would be he was not sure, but he thought he knew. If his deductions were correct, the cabin in which he sat was slowly being filled with one of the most deadly gases in the world, monoxide—an insidious poison, invisible, odourless, but deadly; presently it would induce unconquerable sleepiness that would quickly become a coma that could only end in death.

He glanced at the watch on his instrument-board and saw that he had been in the air nearly forty minutes; if his suspicions were correct, then it was time the gas was making its presence felt. He had not long to wait. Five minutes later, one of the two mice slid slowly from its perch to the floor of the cage and lay still. The other clung desperately to the frail stick for another minute and then collapsed beside its fellow.

Not until he groped into the canvas pocket beside him did Biggles realise how far the poison had worked on him; his movements were sluggish and his power of concentration already weakened. Desperately he held his breath until he had dragged out a bulky object from the pocket and slipped it quickly over his face. It was an ordinary Service gas-mask. He needed both hands to adjust it, and the machine rocked slightly as he released the control-column. So much the better, he reasoned; the unusual behaviour of the aircraft would lend colour to the part he was about to play. A wave of rage swept over him, for he knew now for certain how the two air-line pilots had met their death. Too late poor Makins must have felt the presence of the unseen death, and tried to land. Indeed he had got the machine to the ground, only to collide with the rocks and perish, unable to find strength to climb out of the blazing machine. And yet—Biggles started as a new thought flashed through his mind. Perhaps he had landed safely. Men who were ruthless enough to poison a pilot in the air would not shrink from destroying all possible evidence on the ground. Yes, that was it. It was they who had run the machine into the rocks, and then set fire to it, leaving the helpless pilot in his seat. Biggles trembled for a moment under the cold fury that gripped him, but with an effort he controlled himself and looked downwards and ahead. Karouma lay below and a little to his left; eagerly his eyes swept over the surrounding country and came to rest on two horsemen with two spare horses standing in a shallow depression near the landing-ground. They were the only human beings in sight, and a puzzled expression crept over his face as he realized they were Arabs or natives of some sort. He began to move the column slowly from side to side so that the machine swayed slightly as it flew; his feet moved alternately on the rudder-bar so that his steering became more erratic and a spectator might well have thought that the pilot was allowing the machine to fly itself. He passed on over the aerodrome and then started to return in a wide circle, just as he imagined the two dead air-line pilots might have done.

Then he cut off his engine and started to glide in. His nostrils quivered once as he saw the horsemen begin to move slowly towards the desolate landing-ground.

Steeper and steeper became his dive, with an occasional sideslip as he neared the ground. He pulled out and landed as badly as he dared without deliberately crashing the machine. Bump-bump-bump, it bounced, and then ran to a standstill in a wild, swerving semi-circle. Swiftly he whipped off his gas-mask and thrust it out of sight, and then sprawled across the floor of the cockpit in an attitude of unconsciousness. Almost at once he heard the thud of horses galloping over the sandy earth towards him, and a low laugh of exultation. Through the lashes of his half-closed eyes he saw the cabin-door flung open and a bearded face, surmounted by a turban, appear. "Arabs, eh," he thought, but the next instant he knew he was mistaken.

"O.K.," said a voice. "He's on the floor."

"Never mind about him; get the stuff out," replied his companion. "There's no sense in hanging around. They may have smelt a rat and have another machine following."

Quickly the supposed precious cargo was removed, and with frequent curses loaded up on the restive horses, which, apparently, did not like the proximity of the still-revolving propeller.

"That's the lot," said the first speaker, from the door of the cabin. "What next?"

"Same as the last," was the reply; "it makes a clean finish. If it doesn't catch fire we'll light it; no one'll ever prove anything from what's left."

"Good enough."

Biggles held his breath as the speaker made his way into the cabin and reached over him for the throttle, which he jerked open, and then, before the machine had time to gather speed, sped back and leapt through the open door.

Biggles was up and in his seat in an instant, grabbing for the control-column, feet feeling for the rudder-bar. He was just in time. With stick and rudder flung right over, the machine swung round, the wing-tip missing the rocks by inches. He throttled back a little while he straightened the machine in the opposite direction, and then took off over the heads of the now plunging horses. He caught a fleeting glimpse of the expressions of utter amazement on the faces of the two riders as he passed over them. Glancing back he saw the spurt of flame from a revolver, but he paid little heed to it. Climbing swiftly, he thrust his gloved fist through a side-window of the cabin in order to admit as much fresh air as possible, redonned his gas-mask, and then felt for the key of the wireless equipment. Swiftly he morsed out his message.

It was nearly two hours later, and he was still following the horsemen, whose weary mounts had dropped back from a full gallop to a tired canter, when he saw a curious formation heading towards him. It consisted of the "Vandal," two Service craft, and a troop-carrier. The men on the ground saw them too and pulled up, for there was little hope of escape in the open country. He saw their hands go up as a Service plane swept down, its guns chattering a warning that was not to be ignored. The troop-carrier landed, and a dozen airmen, with rifles at the trail, jumped out. He watched them string out into line and surround the fugitives, and then, beckoning the "Vandal" to follow, turned back towards the landing-ground.

"It wasn't very difficult," he told the Colonel, who had rushed across to him as soon as their wheels touched the ground. "As soon as I spotted that faulty manifold-connection I guessed why poor Dawlish and Makins had tried to land. Just take a look at that." He pointed towards a short piece of tubing behind the manifold. "That leads back into the cabin. Slow, but deadly. It was devilish clever, because the pilot would be almost certain to make for the nearest landing-ground, where, of course, they were waiting. The crash was bound to look like an accident. It was a thousand to one against anybody noticing that little piece of tubing in the tangle of the wreck. We had better take it off now and the machine can be flown back to Cairo. Has Algy got the gold on the 'Vandal'?"

"Yes."

"Good! Then we'll be moving on. If there is any doubt about those two crooks hanging let us know and we'll slip back and give evidence."

CHAPTER 13

THE LAST SHOW

UNDER a leaden-coloured sky the travel-stained amphibian fought its way through a thirty-mile-an-hour headwind across the Channel towards the English coast. From time to time, low, driving clouds blotted out the horizon and embraced the aeroplane in a clammy mist that formed in little globules on the wings, only to be swept away instantly by the swirling slipstream of the propeller.

Biggles, at the control-column, snatched a fleeting glance at Algy, who sat beside him, and forced a grin. "Welcome home!" he yelled above the roar of the engines, and then turned his attention again to the task of keeping the "Vandal" on its course. A grey moving speck in the mist a short distance ahead caught his eye and held it; he recognised it at once as one of the London-to-Paris machines, obviously bound for London from Paris. He knew also that the pilot of the airliner would be in direct wireless communication with Northolt, so he altered his course slightly to follow it. Directional control would take the big machine round or above any really bad weather that lay ahead; it would also steer clear of any traffic outward-bound from Northolt, so he was not displeased at the circumstance.

Both machines were flying low, at about one thousand feet, just under the indigo ceiling, and as the "Vandal" was slightly faster than the other it was not more than a hundred yards behind when the coastline loomed up dimly through the gloom. Biggles recognised the long, deserted arm of Dungeness immediately ahead and took some comfort from the knowledge that they were right on their course.

Then a curious thing happened, a thing he had never seen in all his flying experience. Something, a small flat object, detached itself from the airliner and dropped like a stone through space. He caught his breath sharply as he followed its fall with his eyes, and then stared back at the big machine, half expecting it to crumple up in mid-air. But a second glance revealed the machine still on even keel, apparently unaffected by the loss of a piece of its structure. He looked down again just in time to see the falling object strike the spit of sand a few yards from the water's edge.

For a moment he hesitated, uncertain how to act. If it was a part of the machine that had come adrift, it was obviously his duty to retrieve it, so that whether or not the machine reached the airport safely the technical officers there would at least be aware of exactly what had occurred. Nevertheless he was by no means pleased at having to break his journey and abandon his guide. In the end, duty conquered; he throttled back and glided down towards the bleak stretch of foreshore, lowering his wheels as he did so. The "Vandal" bumped once or twice, grated harshly over some loose pebbles, and then ran to a standstill a hundred yards or so from the spot where the object had struck.

"What's wrong?" inquired Algy anxiously.

"Nothing," replied Biggles tersely. "Hold her; I shan't be a second."

So saying, he jumped down from the cockpit, ran across the sand, found the object without difficulty, and picking it up turned it over and over curiously. It was a flat package about ten inches by six, an inch or so in thickness, wrapped in black paper, with a broad white band pasted round the middle. He realised at once that it was this striking magpie effect that had made it so conspicuous as it lay on the dull yellow sand. There was no address on it, although it was securely tied with a piece of cord as if ready for posting.

The sound of an aero-engine overhead made him look up quickly; it was a single-engine plane, circling as if to land. He waved his hands above his head, assuming that the pilot had seen the "Vandal" on the ground and not unnaturally thought it was in difficulties. Either the pilot did not see, or did not understand his signal, for he cut his engine and began gliding down. Biggles, unwilling to put him to the trouble of an unnecessary landing, darted back to the "Vandal," climbed into his seat, and, swinging round into the wind, took off.

In the air, he jerked his thumb in the direction of the plane, which had taken up a position very close to them.

"He thought we'd force-landed!" he yelled in Algy's ear.

Algy nodded, understanding, and waved a cheery signal of thanks to the pilot of the other machine. Nevertheless, it stayed behind them for some minutes after they had resumed their course for London, and then it suddenly put its nose down and soon left them far behind.

"I'll put this inside!" yelled Biggles, indicating the package, which was lying on his knees. "Take over for a minute." He disappeared into the cabin and returned a few minutes later just as Northolt Airport came into view. The watcher on the control-tower flashed his signal giving them permission to land, and they touched their wheels on an English aerodrome for the first time for many months.

"Well, here we are," observed Biggles. "It seems a long time since we left South America, and we've been a long way round. It's time the old 'Vandal' had a rest; she has certainly done some work. Well, let's get our suitcases; we shall have to clear customs here, I suppose. Smyth, stand by the machine till we come back; we'll fix up accommodation for the machine as soon as we've reported in."

"By the way, what on earth did you pick up when we landed?" asked Algy, suddenly remembering the incident.

"This," replied Biggles, holding up the package. "It either fell overboard or else it was thrown overboard by some silly fool. I'll give it to the Traffic Manager; he ought to know about it. Come on."

With his suitcase in one hand and the package in the other he led the way to the customs barrier.

"Where have you come from?" asked the official.

"Paris."

"Anything to declare?"

"Nothing."

In obedience to the official's request he had just opened his suitcase when he became aware that two men had approached him from behind and were standing at his elbows. He turned sharply and found himself staring into the face of a thick-set man of about fifty years of age.

"Well," asked Biggles, "what is it?"

For a moment the man made no reply. With a swift movement he whipped the package from under Biggles's arm and held it up. "What's this?" he asked shortly.

Now, there are moments when every Englishman, no matter what his rank may be, knows instinctively when he is in the presence of authority, and for Biggles this was one of them. Nevertheless, he bridled under the abrupt question. "What the dickens has that got to do with you?" he snapped.

"I am Detective-Inspector Myhew of Scotland Yard," was the curt reply, and with a quick movement the officer tore a strip from the covering of the package. The tear disclosed a red morocco case and part of a heavily embossed coat-of-arms. "And I arrest you for being concerned with the theft of Lady Nunheaton's pearls," concluded the officer.

"I——"

"And it is my duty to warn you," interrupted the detective imperturbably, "that anything you say may be used as evidence. Better come quietly."

A vice-like grip closed on Biggles's left arm.

Algy stared at the proceedings helplessly.

"But I picked this up on the beach——"

"Yes, quite so," agreed the detective. "Are you coming quietly or——?" He tapped his pocket significantly.

"But this is a scandal," protested Biggles indignantly. "I was just going to hand that package to the Traffic Manager."

"Of course you were," smiled the officer. "Come on, now; get going."

In a daze the two airmen were quietly led through a few idle sightseers in the main hall to a big saloon-car that stood at the entrance.

"I——" stammered Algy.

"I shouldn't talk. Wait till you get to the Yard; you can do all the talking you like then," suggested the officer tersely.

It was nearly dark as the car threaded its way through London's traffic. Rain had started falling in earnest and it seemed to Algy that he had never seen a more depressing spectacle. Soon, for the first time in their lives, the two airmen looked at the gloomy portal of New Scotland Yard, London's famous police-headquarters. A policeman was on duty at the door.

"In you go," said the detective shortly, and still in a daze the two pilots filed past the doorkeeper into a hall. It took them a couple of minutes to realise they were alone.

"Where's that detective chap?" Biggles asked the doorkeeper irritably a few moments later.

"They said they were going to put the car away," was the reply.

It may seem strange, but it took Biggles several seconds to realise that this procedure was not in accordance with what he understood to be the normal method of dealing with suspected persons at police-stations. He returned to the constable on duty.

"What did you say Inspector Myhew said?" he asked.

"Inspector who?"

"Myhew."

The constable looked puzzled. "Never heard of him," he said, shaking his head. "Are you waiting here to see someone?"

Biggles nearly choked. "Good heavens, man, we've just been arrested for stealing Lady Nunheaton's pearls," he snarled, suddenly realising that something was wrong. "You'd better take us to the inspector in charge, and lose no time about it."

Within two minutes Biggles was telling his story to a uniformed inspector in a stiffly furnished office. When he had finished, the inspector pressed a bell, gave some orders in a rapid undertone to the men who answered it, and then returned to the two airmen.

"Well," he said, "it looks to me as if you've been done, and very cleverly. They were smart lads that brought you here. The French police have had a net round Paris for the last week, ever since the pearls were stolen, a net that an ant couldn't get through—so they said. And we've been watching this end. Yet, in spite of that, the thieves managed to get the goods on that aeroplane. Rather than risk having them turned up at Northolt, they dropped them at a pre-arranged spot and had another machine standing by to pick them up. By a million-to-one chance you butted in and lifted the pot, which was a thing they couldn't foresee. The fellows in the other plane took the only course open to them, and it came off. They had to gamble you were going to land at Northolt; in fact, they were pretty sure of it after they had watched you flying towards London. Then they went on, got in ahead of you, put their story over the customs-officer—who can't be blamed, because he knows we've been on the lookout—and then waited for you. It was a cool piece of work to arrest you, though; yet they had to do something. Having got the goods back they had to get rid of you, and that wasn't so easy. If they had made one slip you might have spotted something was wrong and started asking awkward questions. They had to come to London, anyway, so they had the nerve to drop you here, the easiest place to get rid of you. Well, it's tough luck for you two. I suppose you know the insurance people have offered two thousand pounds reward for the return of the necklace?" concluded the officer.

Biggles started. "How much?" he ejaculated. "Say that again."

"Two thousand pounds."

"Does that still hold good?"

"Of course."

Biggles put his hand into his trousers-pocket and drew out a long double string of pearls that gleamed whitely in the artificial light. "That's fine," he said. "Where do we collect the cash?"

For a moment the inspector stared unbelievingly at the jewels; then he turned a suspicious eye on the pilot. "What's the idea?" he said coldly. "What are you trying to put across me?"

"I've told you the plain, sober truth, and presently I'll prove it, if you like," answered Biggles simply. "When those jewels were stolen I was in Cairo, and by my log-book and carnets I can account for every minute of my time till I booked out from Le Bourget, Paris. You'll find my wheel-tracks on the sand at Dungeness. The only thing I omitted from my story was that when we were in the air I stepped back into the cabin to look at what I had picked up. My mechanic will confirm that; he was there. I guessed that something was wrong, particularly as that single-engine plane followed us, so I did up the parcel again, but I kept the pearls in my pocket. The crooks took me in completely, I admit, but they made a bigger mistake. When they saw the red-leather case it did not occur to them for one moment that it might have been opened in the air. They knew I hadn't opened it on the ground, either at Dungeness or at Northolt, because they were watching me all the time. So they took it for granted that the beads were still inside. They weren't, and they've either kicked themselves to death by now or else they are hanging about outside waiting for us to come out."

The inspector started. "Gosh! You may be right," he said, making for the door.

"And we'd better see about putting our machine to bed," observed Biggles to Algy. "Smyth will be getting anxious. And then we'll have a rest ourselves; we've earned one, I think."